CHOPPER ATTACK

Aloft in the blue MAX-2, Frank pointed to the southwest. "Look!" Down below was the MAX-1. As he and Joe watched, their quarry hit the turboboost, and the MAX-1 rocketed away at supersonic speed.

"There are the two Apaches," Joe said, indicating two predatory helicopters swooping toward them. "They must have spotted him, too."

"Too bad they didn't catch him," said Frank. "I guess it's up to us. Let's go."

Frank started to bank in pursuit of the MAX-1, but the two Apaches kept coming, straight for the MAX-2.

"What's wrong with those chopper jocks? Can't they tell the difference between the MAX-1 and the MAX-2?" shouted Frank. Then realization dawned on his face. "Didn't someone tell them to go after the *red* one?"

As if in answer, the lead chopper launched a pair of missiles straight at them!

"They've mistaken us for the bad guys!" Joe yelled. "Let's get out of here!"

Books in THE HARDY BOYS CASEFILES® Series

Available from ARCHWAY Paperbacks

THE HARDY BOYS NO. 47

CASEFILES

FLIGHT INTO DANGER

FRANKLIN W. DIXON

AN ARCHWAY PAPERBACK
Published by POCKET BOOKS
New York   London   Toronto   Sydney   Tokyo   Singapore

This book is a work of fiction. Names, characters, places and incidents are either the product of the author's imagination or are used fictitiously. Any resemblance to actual events or locales or persons, living or dead is entirely coincidental.

An ARCHWAY PAPERBACK *Original*

 An Archway Paperback published by
POCKET BOOKS, a division of Simon & Schuster
1230 Avenue of the Americas, New York, NY 10020

Copyright © 1991 by Simon & Schuster
Cover art copyright © 1991 Brian Kotzky
Produced by Mega-Books of New York, Inc.

ISBN: 0-671-70044-8

First Archway Paperback printing January 1991

10 9 8 7 6 5 4 3 2 1

Printed in the U.S.A.

IL 7+

FLIGHT INTO DANGER

Chapter

1

"COME ON, JOE, I know you're faking it. You can't be that sleepy. Let's go!" Frank Hardy nudged his brother in the ribs and turned off the ignition.

"Am, too," Joe grumbled, hunkering deeper into the passenger seat of their black, customized van. The quilt their aunt Gertrude had stitched for Joe when he was eight was pulled tight around his neck. Frank shook his head as he watched Joe duck his head under the warm cover and pretend to be asleep.

Not giving up, Frank undid his seat belt and got out of the van. He walked around the front to the other side and yanked the passenger door open. Joe tumbled out into the frigid January morning.

"I'll get you for that, Frank," Joe complained as he lurched to his feet, brushing gravel off his blue jeans. "I have better things to do on a cold Saturday morning than freeze outside."

"Like what?" Frank slapped his arms to warm himself. "Sleep late? Watch Looney Tunes reruns? This is going to be Bayport's best air show ever. You'll love it!"

Joe shivered miserably and hunched his shoulders against the cold. He couldn't understand Frank's enthusiasm as he watched him slam the door of the van and bound off across Bayport Airfield's windy parking lot, his steaming breath leaving a momentary trail behind him.

"No warm bed for me," Joe muttered, pulling his wool hat down over his tousled blond hair and bracing his muscular, six-foot frame against the freezing wind. "No hot cocoa. No cartoons."

"Right on time, Callie," Joe heard Frank call to Frank's pretty girlfriend, who was pulling up. "I thought you might decide to miss the show."

"No way." Callie Shaw laughed and tossed her blond hair over her shoulder. "I remember how terrific the planes were last year."

How can two people be so cheery at eight o'clock on a ten-degree morning? Joe wondered, walking slowly over to join them. So what if the sky was blue and the sun was shining? It was still cold, and the wind was fierce. He gave the warm van one last sorrowful glance, then hustled the rest of the distance to Frank and Callie.

The Bayport Airfield, bigger than many other private ones, sat surrounded by fields about five miles outside of Bayport. Several hangars stood at the far end of its single runway. Beside the hangars was a small pilots' clubhouse. The wind sock attached to the roof was stretched straight by the wind.

Right then the field looked bright and festive, with streamers tied to the storm fence that encircled it. Near the hangars, the tails of several new, brightly painted airplanes could be seen, and several vintage biplanes were nearby. In between were airplanes of all shapes and sizes.

Joe caught up with Frank and Callie just as they reached the main gate. "Hi, Joe," Callie said as Frank was buying their tickets from a big, white-haired man in a down jacket and gloves. "Isn't it a beautiful, crisp morning?" she said teasingly.

"Not you, too, Callie. Maybe you can tell me why Bayport always schedules its air show in the middle of winter."

"You know why," Callie said with exaggerated patience. "It's Greenland Day! Sixty-five years ago Ethan Lachlan took off from here on his record-breaking flight to the far north, and—"

"Yeah, okay, I do know, but I still don't understand why we have to act crazy just because some old guy—"

Joe's complaint was cut off as Frank gave a whoop and ran for the cluster of old biplanes and single-wing planes parked on the runway. Joe watched, amazed that Frank's slim, quarterback's body seemed unaffected by the cold. Then he realized Frank was just too excited to feel it. Joe had to remind himself that Frank's weakness for planes was almost as major as his for cars and motorcycles.

Every year Frank insisted on getting to the air show early to beat the crowds, and every year Joe griped and grumbled. Well, he decided, he might as well stop grumbling, because there wasn't a chance of getting out of there before lunchtime.

"Those really are beautiful," Callie said as she and Joe approached the old planes. "Look at those wooden propellers. I wonder why they didn't break in the middle of a flight?"

"Are you kidding?" Frank answered, ducking under the nose of a bright red Stearman to stroke the varnished smoothness of the plane's Sensenich Brothers propeller. "This thing is laminated oak. The only thing that can break this propeller is flying it into the ground. And that big Wright radial engine will fly till it falls out of the plane.''

''Not too many people here,'' Joe remarked. He shoved his hands in his jacket pockets and eyed the crowd. ''Nobody we know, anyway. Chet Morton, Tony Prito, Phil Cohen—they're all tucked into nice warm beds, dreaming of scrambled eggs for breakfast.''

Callie laughed. ''Your loyalty will be rewarded, Joe,'' she said. ''Look how happy Frank is. Doesn't that warm your heart?''

Frank had walked over to a group of World War II fighters and climbed into the cockpit of a P-51 Mustang. He grinned down at them like a kid and made a thumbs-up gesture, the wind whipping his thick brown hair straight back.

''Oh, well,'' Joe muttered to Callie. ''If you can't fight 'em, join 'em.'' He hopped up on the wing of the Mustang and leaned in toward his big brother. ''Okay, spill it,'' he said. ''What's so special about this one?''

''Special? Are you kidding? The engine's a twelve hundred horsepower Rolls-Royce twelve-cylinder. In its heyday, this baby could outrun, outclimb, outturn, and outfly any plane in the air. The P-51 was the best fighter during the Second World War.''

''Not bad.'' Joe looked at the airplane with more respect. ''Must have been a shaky ride, though.''

"Who cares?" Frank leapt out of the cockpit, his eyes shining. "That's part of the fun. Speaking of fun, look at this one!" He jumped to the ground and hurried to the next plane in line, Joe and Callie following him.

Frank was referring to a twin-engined war bird that looked to Joe as if it had been made by crashing two planes together. Not only did it have two engines, it had two tails and two fuselages connected by a single wing. "This is a P-38. The Japanese called it the fork-tailed devil because of its twin tails. The Americans loved having two engines because it meant that they could lose one and still limp home. And there's a Corsair!"

Frank turned toward the gleaming navy blue fighter with its wings folded up over its cockpit. "It was a navy fighter and—" Just then he realized that Joe and Callie were laughing at his enthusiasm. For a second he glared at them. Then he shrugged, saying, "If you don't want to know, then I'm not going to tell you."

Joe and Callie said that they did want to hear, so Frank continued talking as they moved down the line of airplanes. Finally they reached an area where the newest models were on view. Joe noticed manufacturers' sales representatives standing in front of each plane, ready to explain its unique features.

"Oh, look, Frank." Callie tugged on his arm

and pointed to a field beyond the runway. "Hot-air balloon rides! Let's buy tickets for later this afternoon."

Frank didn't hear her. He had already drifted over to the first of the new planes. A salesman approached him and handed him a brochure.

"Forget it, Callie," Joe said with a grin. "With his pilot's license, you've got as much chance of getting him into a balloon as I have of getting breakfast."

A high-pitched shriek split the air above them. Joe and Callie looked up to see a blue jet streaking low over the runway. Five just like it followed quickly in formation before disappearing immediately. Frank turned and shouted to them over the roar. "The Blue Angels. They're amazing, right?"

"Yep, they are." Callie nodded to Frank, then turned to Joe. "And after the Blue Angels, there are the experimental planes, and after them, the vintage air show. Suddenly I wonder if we'll eat at all today."

Frank was already at the very end of the runway, at what was considered the best exhibit at the fair. The company that sponsored it had rented an entire hangar. A sign near the entrance read, "International Expeditors, Ltd. Custom Flying Machines. San Diego, California."

"Wow." Frank ducked inside the hangar and gave a low whistle. "Look at the size of that thing." Inside was a large plane, the largest at the show, in fact. Joe couldn't understand what made it so interesting to his brother other than its size.

"So, it's big." Joe joined Frank beside the plane and reached up to stroke its gleaming side. "Is that a reason to fall in love?"

"No, dummy. This plane's remarkable," Frank explained as he stepped back to admire the aircraft. "This thing could revolutionize air transport. It's a STOL."

"A what?" Callie asked.

"*STOL* stands for Short Takeoff and Landing. Most planes this big need a long runway," Frank explained. "Longer than we have here in Bayport. But this baby can almost go straight up and come straight down. It can take off and land practically anywhere."

Callie nodded. "That's good, huh?"

"It's great! It means that remote towns and villages can move stuff in and out cheaply. It had been impossible to develop a really workable STOL—especially a big one—until now. The guy who designed this must be a genius."

Frank picked up a brochure from a stack near the front of the plane. He flipped through it. "Aha," he said triumphantly. "I thought so."

"What?" asked Callie.

"This says the designer is Max Lachlan. I should have known."

"Your friend Ray Adamec works for him, right?" asked Joe. "Is that why he called you last night?"

"Well, he told me to be sure not to miss the show today. But he wouldn't tell me why exactly. This must be part of the reason."

"Is Max any relation to Ethan Lachlan, our famous record-breaking pilot?" Callie asked.

"His son," answered Frank. "He's lived in Bayport all his life, even though every major aircraft manufacturer has tried to woo him away."

Frank glanced at his watch. "It's almost time. Ray told me to be at the Lachlan Air Design hangar this morning. He said he had something really exciting to show us. That must be the rest of the reason for his call."

As they left the International Expeditors hangar, Joe pointed out a large crowd gathering around another hangar. "Looks like something's up over there."

"That's Lachlan's hangar," Frank said as they started down the runway. "Ray works for him as an engineer occasionally, he told me, but mostly he's a test pilot." He ran a hand through his dark hair. "I wish he'd kept in touch more. I've heard from him once or twice since he joined the navy two years ago."

"How come he's out of the navy now?" Joe asked. "Isn't it too soon for his hitch to be up?"

"I was wondering that, too. I asked him about it last night, but he changed the subject." A puzzled look crossed Frank's face.

"Uh-oh." Callie frowned up at him. "I know that look. You think there's a mystery here, don't you?"

"I don't know. It's just that—"

"What else do you know about his new boss?" asked Joe.

"Lachlan? Just that he's the best and that he's a hothead, too. I hear his temper's so bad, no one likes to work for him. He designs on his own because he has to, but the stuff he designs is ten times better than anything else out there."

"Like what?" Callie asked.

"Like that STOL we just saw, and components for the space shuttle. Only his designs for those were rejected at the last minute by NASA. I read somewhere that he called the NASA people total idiots. But that was a while ago."

"Sounds like a great guy," Callie said.

"Ray seems to get along with him all right," Frank answered.

"Look." Joe gestured toward the crowd. Several television reporters and camerapeople were bustling around expectantly. "Whatever Lachlan's got up his sleeve, he's called the press out to see it.''

Frank led Joe and Callie toward a grandstand that had been set up near Lachlan's hangar. Several local dignitaries were already seated there. Frank recognized the mayor, Chief Collig of the Bayport Police, and a few important businesspeople.

"Poor guys," Joe remarked slyly. "Look how cold they are. Their breath is freezing in front of their faces.''

Just as they were seated, a large man in his fifties stepped up to the microphone. His windbreaker was half unzipped, and his tanned, leathery complexion made him look as if he'd flown straight in from Jamaica. Frank gaped at him admiringly. This man looked anything but cold.

"Max Lachlan?" Callie asked.

"The man himself." Frank listened as the bearlike man started to speak. He gestured broadly with his large, strong hands. His thick white hair tumbled over his ears. All eyes in the crowd were on him. He looked exactly like the genius he obviously was.

"Ladies and gentlemen," he rumbled in a low, gravelly voice. "Thank you so much for attending our little exhibition. This is an important day for me, and I'm very happy to have someone special here to share it with me."

Joe yawned as Lachlan stepped back to al-

11

low the audience to see the someone who was seated behind him. Joe became interested at once when he saw the beautiful dark-haired girl Lachlan was pointing to. She wore faded jeans and an emerald green bomber jacket. As the audience applauded and whistled, she rose, smiling tentatively.

Joe whistled. "Who's *she?*" he asked. "Very impressive."

As if in answer, Lachlan said, "My daughter, Moira, who is making her old man very proud by following in his footsteps. She's studying aeronautics at MIT!"

The crowd applauded again. After Moira waved and sat down, Lachlan grew serious.

"Folks, Bayport has been very good to me and my family. I've always wanted to give something back to this town. Now I have a chance to do just that. We've all dreamed of the day when an aircraft would be as easy to own and operate as the family car. Well, that day is here! May I present—the MAX-1!"

Frank looked up at the sky along with everyone else. Far up but falling fast was a tiny red dot. Frank squinted at the dot and watched it grow quickly larger as it plummeted toward the earth. Whatever the MAX-1 was, it was really fast, tiny, and quiet. As hard as Frank strained his ears, he could not hear the brilliant red aircraft's engine. As he watched the plane grow larger, he began to worry.

The MAX-1 leveled out over the runway and streaked toward the grandstands filled with early-morning risers. It hurtled lower, then Joe yelled, "It's too low. It's going to crash!"

The crowd started to scatter. "The pilot's lost control!" Callie shouted as Joe yanked her off her bleacher seat. "It's coming in *too* fast!"

Callie screamed as the red craft continued on its course—headed straight for them!

Chapter

2

WHILE THE CROWD continued to disperse, only Frank Hardy remained seated. Max Lachlan, he noted, hadn't budged from the microphone stand. He was standing calmly with his arms folded, a small smile on his lips. Obviously, Frank realized, all was not what it seemed.

Frank yelled for Joe and Callie. "Something's up," he told them.

"I agree," Joe said. "This looks planned!"

An instant before the MAX-1 would crash into the grandstand, its engines began to whine furiously. To everyone's amazement, the red aircraft stopped dead in the air a few yards in front of the stand. It hovered there like a giant dragonfly, its engines thrumming quietly.

14

The crowd slowly realized that *this* was the surprise. They stared up at the red plane. Frank hardly heard their murmur of stunned appreciation because he was too busy taking in the beautiful saucer-shaped craft as it slowly descended, straight down.

Max Lachlan grinned as the MAX-1 settled gently onto the runway in front of the grandstand. He threw his arms wide and announced into the microphone, "Ladies and gentlemen, I give you—the MAX-1!"

The crowd's polite applause quickly turned into a roar of approval. Television crews and ordinary onlookers surged forward as the canopy of the red aircraft popped open. Minicams trained on the pilot as he stood up. He pulled his helmet off. He was a young man with dark blond hair and a mustache. His wide grin matched Max's.

"It's Ray!" Frank shouted. He began to thread his way through the crowd toward his friend. Joe and Callie followed.

"It's my pleasure," Max continued into the microphone, "to present to you Bayport's own Ray Adamec. The finest test pilot a designer could ask for—*and* my future son-in-law!"

Joe cast a quick glance at Moira. Sure enough, she was beaming at Ray, her eyes alive with excitement.

"Why are the good ones always taken?" Joe muttered.

"Now, Joe," Callie said, "I'm sure you'll find somebody to fall in love with before the day's over."

Joe watched Moira walk over to the MAX-1 and hug her fiancé. They made a very handsome couple. As they smiled for the cameras, Ray spotted Frank in the crowd. He waved excitedly and gestured toward the MAX-1.

"Frank Hardy! Like my new toy? I told you it was something else!"

Frank laughed. The security guards, who had formed a protective circle around the plane, opened a space for Frank, Joe, and Callie to move in next to Ray. Frank gave the pilot a big bear hug.

"Ray, you know my brother, Joe," Frank said.

"Good to see you." Joe shook Ray's hand warmly.

"And this is Callie Shaw," Frank said.

"My pleasure," said Ray. He shook Callie's hand. Then he put an arm around Moira. "I guess Moira's dad already introduced her, right?"

"Don't I know you?" Callie asked the older girl.

"I think so," Moira said. "You go to Bayport High, right?"

"That's it! You were captain of the cheerleading squad three years ago."

"That's where I know you from," said Joe. He shook Moira's hand and grinned. "Never could forget a pretty face."

Just then another pretty girl worked her way through the crowd. "Hey, Moira!" she cried.

Moira turned and the guards let the new girl through.

"Jill!" Moira said. "You made it."

"I wouldn't have missed it for the world—especially since my editor made this my assignment."

"You're a reporter?" Joe instantly forgot about Moira as he smiled at her short, perky friend. Jill's jet black hair contrasted well with her green eyes, and Joe liked her enthusiasm.

"Yes," she answered with an impish smile. "And I already know who you are—Joe Hardy. Half of Bayport's famous crime-solving team. Second only to your father, Detective Fenton Hardy." She looked around at the others. "Wow, nothing but celebrities on all sides of me!"

"See, Joe?" Callie remarked in a low voice. "There's still a chance to fall in love before the sun goes down."

"So tell me all about this MAX-1, Ray," Jill said as she clicked her pen open. "How did Lachlan come up with such an incredible design?"

"He's a genius," Ray said simply, then started to tell the story of the MAX-1. Frank hardly heard a word his friend was saying. He was walking around the magnificent machine, trying to understand how it had done the impossible things he had just seen it do.

The streamlined craft was nearly twenty feet long and ten feet wide. The engines were clustered around the passenger compartment. The plane had no wings—rather, the whole body was wing. Frank realized how much like some early space shuttle designs this was. What were they called? he wondered. Lifting bodies?

Ray's voice broke through Frank's concentration. "The MAX has six small jet engines," he was saying. "These two on either side of the vertical stabilizer are fixed. They provide the thrust. But the other four rotate."

Frank followed Ray's gaze to the engines arranged on either end of the plane. Two were in front of the cabin, and two were behind.

"So they can provide lift or thrust," Frank said.

"Right," said Moira. "They're what allows the MAX-1 to take off and land straight up and down. It can hover and then take off like a shot. It can even fly backward."

Ray grinned at Frank. "You wouldn't believe what it's like to fly," he said. "It's easier to handle than a Harrier jump-jet and nearly as fast—and in a package less than half the size!"

Jill hastily scribbled notes. "What's a Harrier jump-jet?"

"It's a British fighter plane," Frank told her. "Our marines have them, too. The British used them in the Falklands War. A Harrier can lift straight off the deck of a ship, soar like a bat, stop still, and change direction. All in a matter of seconds."

"But our plane is better," Moira insisted.

"And this is no fighter," Ray pointed out. "It's the best sports car in the world!"

He lifted the bubble canopy and showed them the cabin. Frank moved forward eagerly to have a look.

It did look almost like a car interior. Frank ran a hand over the plush bucket seats and the dual-control dashboard.

Suddenly Ray had an inspiration.

"Hey, Frank. Did you ever get that pilot's license you were working for?"

"Passed it on the first try."

Ray grinned. "Great! Tell me what you see on the passenger seat?"

Frank's eyes widened. "An extra helmet—"

"Put it on. We're going for a spin."

"Ray, shouldn't you ask Dad first?" Moira said a bit nervously.

Ray shrugged. "He won't mind, Mo. Besides, look—he's surrounded by reporters. It would take an hour just to get him and ask permission."

Grinning, the lanky pilot turned to Frank. "Come on, pal, let's go!"

"What about me?" Joe asked. Suddenly he had become very interested in airplanes.

"Sorry, Joe. There are only two seats. Maybe I can take you up later."

Frank waved goodbye to Callie and climbed into the passenger seat. He couldn't remember when he'd been so excited. If the MAX-1 was even half as good as Ray and Moira said, he was in for an incredible ride.

As Ray joined Frank in the cockpit, the guards moved the crowd farther from the plane. One man pushed his way forward. He was small and balding, and his eyes were fixed on one of the rear engines.

Jill stood next to Joe and snapped pictures of the plane. When the small man noticed her camera, he suddenly backed up. Jill pointed him out to Joe.

"That was funny. That guy seemed scared of my camera," she said.

By that time the man had disappeared into the crowd. Jill frowned. "He was just here."

Joe shrugged. "Probably just curious."

As Ray was lowering the bubble top, he began explaining the MAX-1's controls to Frank.

"Max designed this so anyone could fly it," he said. "Everything is computerized. The controls are simpler than those on an ordinary plane or helicopter. It's almost like a car with automatic transmission. Ready?"

Frank grinned as Ray flipped six switches on the control panel to start the engines. They pulsed and hummed as he ran through a computerized checklist that popped up on one of several screens on the instrument panel. Finally Ray gripped the joystick, and the MAX-1 rose straight off the ground, its engines whining.

As the MAX-1 shot up, Frank whooped with excitement.

Joe watched the red aircraft soar upward and sighed—he wanted a ride in it. It looked more like an air-based motorcycle than a standard plane.

He glanced toward the grandstand. Lachlan was looking up, astonished, his eyes round, his face red. He hadn't expected Ray to offer joyrides to his friends.

"Look at that," Joe said to Jill, pointing toward Lachlan. The designer had excused himself from the crowd clustered around him and moved back to the podium. He gripped its edges, his face dangerously red now. "Looks like the famous Lachlan temper's on red alert."

Aboard the MAX-1, Frank laughed as the aircraft darted first one way, then another. Its banks of tiny computer screens lit up with information on altitude, flight angle, velocity, and a dozen other things Frank hadn't wondered about.

"All this flight information is fed straight into

an automatic guidance system for the aircraft,'' Ray explained. "I don't even have to worry about it. All I have to do is point the plane in the right direction, hit the throttles, and the computers tell the engines, the ailerons, and the stabilizers how to make the plane do what I want.''

"I can't believe it." Frank shook his head in admiration. "It moves like it's a part of you."

"It just about is by now," Ray said with a chuckle. "I've put more hours into this baby than I have into sleeping over the past few months.''

A few moments later Ray turned to his friend and smiled. "Frank, old buddy, take the controls," he said.

Frank stared at him. "No joke?"

"No joke. I'll back you up. Just give her a try!"

Frank didn't need any more encouragement. He gripped the controls. As Ray talked him through it, he made the MAX-1 dip and swoop, climb, hover, and dart. "Wow!" he cried. "This is even more fun than I thought!"

The two friends laughed as Frank eased the craft into a slow, graceful turn.

"What did I tell you?" Ray said, slapping his younger friend on the back.

"You were right!" Frank answered. "This is the best toy in the world!"

Then suddenly the MAX-1 lurched and shuddered. Frank glanced at Ray for reassurance, but Ray was staring at the control board. He looked stricken.

There was a loud thump, and the aircraft lurched again. Frank grabbed the dashboard and held on. With a jolt, all three engines on the left switched off and the plane veered sharply to one side.

"What's going on?" Frank shouted as the MAX-1 went into a spinning dive.

"I don't know!" Ray flipped switches frantically, trying to regain control of the craft. "But we're in big trouble!"

For an instant Frank caught a view of the earth below. The airfield lay beneath them like a toy-size model. The people gaping up at them looked no bigger than ants. The engines shrieked as the plane plummeted toward them like a rock.

The MAX-1 was going to crash. And this time it was no stunt!

Chapter

3

FRANK HARDY could keep his cool in most dangerous situations, but his composure was nothing compared to the way Ray instantly became the professional. Frank was amazed at how calmly his friend methodically but quickly tested each control.

"Throw that switch over there, Frank," Ray ordered. Frank did as he was told. Nothing happened.

"No good." Ray frowned. "Let's try something else."

"Like what? We're crashing!" Frank said. He couldn't contain his anxiety a second longer. The MAX-1 was spinning like a top. The engines on the left side remained useless. The aircraft swooped toward the earth, then spun into a stomach-heaving loop up to the sky again. It would have been the world's greatest roller-coaster ride—if they weren't about to die.

On the ground Callie and Jill clung to each other, staring in horror at the spinning plane. "What's happening?" Joe yelled in frustration. "Can't somebody do something?"

All around them people were screaming and running for cover. News photographers and a TV crew had trained their cameras on the MAX-1, recording every terrible moment. "Turn off your cameras!" Joe yelled, but the newspeople ignored him.

Joe glanced around wildly. There must be something he could do to save his brother. His eyes went to Max Lachlan and locked on him. Joe would have expected the man to look panicky as his triumph fell to the earth. Instead he was standing calmly at the podium, his hands deep in his pockets, watching the MAX-1 with an intense, thoughtful expression. His way of coping, Joe decided.

Inside the aircraft, Frank was pounding the dashboard. "Isn't there anything we can do?" he yelled at the young man in the pilot's seat.

Then, as suddenly as they'd shut down, the engines on the left side of the aircraft thrummed to life. Frank stared at Ray as he calmly took control again. Then he leaned back against the passenger seat.

"Whoo!" Frank gasped. "You did it!"

Ray shook his head. Now that the emergency was over, it was clear that he'd been badly frightened, too. Beads of sweat stood out on his tanned forehead. His hand was shaking on the joystick.

"I don't think so, buddy," he said. "Nothing *I* did worked. Let's get this bird back on the ground before anything else happens. Then we can try to figure out what went wrong."

He played the controls, and the MAX-1 descended smoothly. It settled onto the airstrip in front of the grandstand as though nothing unusual had happened.

Frank jumped out of the plane as soon as Ray popped the canopy. It felt good to be on solid ground again! Callie ran up to hug him, tears running down her face. Looking over her shoulder, Frank met Joe's eyes. The brothers grinned sheepishly at each other.

"Some show," Joe said gruffly. "You really warmed up the crowd, if that was what you wanted."

Before Frank could reply, he and Ray were besieged by reporters. Jill Stern asked the one question on everybody's mind. "Ray," she said, pushing through the crowd to where he stood with his arm around Moira. "What happened up there? Sabotage?"

"It wasn't sabotage," barked a gruff voice before Ray could open his mouth. "It was incompetence!"

Frank turned around to see Max Lachlan shouldering his massive frame through the crowd. His face was red with fury. He confronted Ray angrily.

"I thought you knew how to fly that thing," he shouted. "And who said you could take this kid for a joyride?"

"I can fly the MAX-1 better than anyone," Ray answered heatedly. "I don't know what happened up there, but it wasn't my fault! Maybe it was a *design* error!"

Now Max Lachlan exploded. "You're saying *I'm* responsible? Why, you—"

His right hand flashed out, and his heavy fist met Ray's shoulder.

Ray leapt for his employer as onlookers cried out in surprise. But Joe and Frank grabbed Ray before he could throw a punch, and several men in the crowd held on to Max Lachlan.

As they were hauled away from each other, Lachlan yelled, "You don't work for me anymore! You're fired!"

"I already quit," Ray shouted back. "Find some other fool to fly that deathtrap!"

*   *   *

Frank, Joe, Callie, and their three friends from that day's adventure were glad to be at Mr. Pizza that night. Frank never thought tomato sauce and pepperoni could smell so good. He handed a second slice to Callie. Ray, Moira, and Joe sat stuffing themselves across the table, and Jill Stern was sipping a giant-size soda on the other side of Frank.

"This is great," Joe said, patting his stomach and leaning back in his chair. "A perfect reward for a hard day's work. Too bad Mom, Dad, and Aunt Gertrude are in Maine and can't hear about Frank's adventure."

"You'd better not be the one to tell them, little brother," Frank said, pointing with his pizza at Joe. "Mom's done enough worrying about us lately."

"It is good to be alive," Ray chimed in, lifting the last piece of pizza. "I say we order dessert after this."

"No more, please!" Moira held up her hands in surrender. "We'd be lucky if a 747 could lift us off the ground after all that pizza."

They all laughed, and Ray, giving in to the majority opinion, put down his slice and reached for his wallet. "Okay, okay," he said. "This one's on me. I owe you guys for the scare you got, after all."

"Are you sure you want to?" Frank said

hesitantly. "I mean, can you afford it now that you don't have a job?"

Ray looked at him blankly. Then he turned to Moira, and the two of them began to laugh.

"What's so funny?" Joe asked, echoing his brother's confusion. "I've never seen anyone so happy about being fired."

"He wasn't fired," Moira explained. "Not really. You have to know my dad to understand."

"Every time something goes wrong, he fires me," Ray explained. "By tomorrow he'll be so caught up trying to figure out why the MAX-1 malfunctioned that he'll need my help. He won't even remember our fight." He shook his head. "After working with him for four months, I know to expect only the unexpected."

"Well, you do know he's a hothead, and you expect him to boil over fast," Moira said.

"His wasn't the only temper that flared up," Callie pointed out with a smile.

Ray's face reddened. "It wouldn't be the first time my temper got me in trouble," he admitted. "I guess you could say Max and I are a lot alike."

"Is that why you're not in the navy anymore?" Jill asked casually.

There was a moment of awkward silence as Ray met Jill's gaze.

"Are you asking as a friend or as a reporter?"

Before Jill could answer, the waitress arrived

with their check, and the tension of the moment was broken. Ray made a big show of paying for the pizza, but, Joe noticed, he never answered Jill's question.

As they began putting on their coats and moving toward the door, Moira and Ray said goodbye. "I'm going to call my dad," Moira explained. "I want to see how he's feeling."

"And if he's talking to me yet," Ray added, grinning.

Joe waited until they were out of earshot before turning to his older brother. "Something's up," he said.

Frank looked uncomfortable and nodded.

"There are two major questions to answer here," Joe went on, lost in thought. "The first is, what happened to the MAX-1? The second, which Ray neatly avoided, is why is he a civilian when he should still be in the navy?"

"Uh-oh," said Callie, who was listening in on the brothers' conversation along with Jill. "You're planning on solving these two mysteries, aren't you?"

Joe gave her a small smile. Frank frowned guiltily. He didn't like the idea of spying on his old friend, Ray.

"And I'm going to miss it!" Callie exclaimed. She sounded so mad that Jill and the brothers had to laugh. "I'm leaving for Florida with my parents tomorrow morning. I'll be gone all week.''

''Don't worry, Callie,'' Jill assured her happily. ''I'll tell you all about it.'' She turned her gaze on the Hardys, who were eyeing her in surprise. ''We *will* be working on this together, won't we, guys?''

Before Frank could tell her they weren't going to work together on anything, Joe interrupted. His attention was focused across the dining room, but he spoke to Jill. ''Remember that guy you saw by the MAX-1?'' He gestured toward a small table in the corner. ''Is that him?''

Jill turned to look. The little, balding man, who had been studying the group throughout their meal, instantly got up to leave and bolted. ''It sure is!'' Jill said excitedly.

''You think he had something to do with the near accident?'' asked Frank.

''Only one way to find out,'' Joe answered under his breath.

The Hardys rushed together toward the exit just as the little man hurried through the door that led directly out to the parking lot. Once outside, Frank and Joe raced into the parking lot to look around.

''Where'd he go?'' Joe demanded. The huge mall parking lot was almost deserted. Mr. Pizza was open after the rest of the mall closed.

Just then Frank heard the noise of an engine revving.

"What's that?" Frank whirled toward the source of the noise.

A pair of headlights switched on to high, momentarily blinding both Hardys. With a roar of its engine, a big gray sedan hurtled across the parking lot straight at Frank and Joe.

"Watch out!" Frank yelled. "It's coming at us!" Frank's arm went out, knocking Joe out of the vehicle's path.

"Frank!" Joe yelled, stumbling to his feet. "Move, before he runs you down!"

Chapter

4

"UNNNH!" FRANK GASPED as Joe tackled him, knocking him out of the path of the oncoming car. Frank's first impulse was to run after the car, but his foot slipped on a patch of ice as he tried to get up. He stumbled and fell back onto his knees. The gray sedan was out of the lot by the time he had gotten to his feet.

"Are you okay?" Callie shouted. She and Jill were outside now, staring at Frank and Joe. Ray and Moira had just joined the girls.

"Yeah, I think so." Frank looked embarrassed. "He clipped me on my shoulder, but I think it's just a bruise."

"Did you get the license plate number?" Joe asked.

"Sorry—I was a little preoccupied," Frank answered sarcastically.

Joe shook his head. "Excuses, excuses," he said to Frank. Then added under his breath, "*Now* do you think we might have a mystery or two on our hands?"

Frank frowned, careful not to look in Ray's direction as his old friend approached. "Maybe you're right."

"Don't say anything," Joe warned him just as the others joined them. "Who knows who's in on it by now?"

The next morning, Joe heard the knocking first. He opened one eye and poked his head out from under the mound of blankets on his bed. Why didn't someone answer?

Oh, that's right, he reminded himself. It's just the two of us in the house this week.

Freedom from parents brought responsibility with it, and Joe forced himself to check his alarm clock. It was 8:35. He rolled over and looked out the window. A light snow fell silently and dusted the treetops.

The knocking grew louder. "All right, I'm coming," Joe grumbled, but he burrowed his way deeper under the blankets. By the time the unknown caller decided to ring the door bell, Joe was sound asleep again.

Frank was already awake and ready for the

day, but since he was in the shower, he didn't hear the knocking. When he turned off the water and heard the door bell, he grabbed his robe and ran for the door.

"Didn't you hear the bell?" he yelled in at Joe as he passed his room.

"Uh-huh," came a muffled voice from under the blankets.

"So wake up already!" Frank demanded, bounding downstairs to the front door. "It's almost nine!"

When Frank opened the door, he found a very cold Moira Lachlan.

"Frank!" she sobbed. Her eyes were red from crying, and two tear streaks ran down her cheeks. "He's gone!"

"Take it easy, Moira." Frank ushered her in and closed the door against the frigid blast behind her. "Who's gone?"

"Ray!" She sniffled, as she dug a tissue out of her pocket to blow her nose. "He's disappeared —and he's stolen the MAX-1!"

It didn't take Joe long to get up and dress once he heard the news. Within minutes he and Frank, both in jeans and sweatshirts, were in the kitchen with Moira, sipping hot cocoa. Frank was relieved that Moira was more relaxed now. She spoke calmly, but she still looked worried.

"Last night after we left the restaurant," she

explained, "Ray dropped me off at home. He promised to call first thing this morning." She paused, collected herself, then continued.

"This morning when the phone rang, it was my dad, not Ray. He said he'd gone to the hangar early to start working on the MAX-1—but it was gone." She looked from Frank to Joe, wide-eyed.

"I drove to Ray's place to see if he knew what had happened. There was no sign of him. Now my dad's sure Ray faked yesterday's malfunction to get the MAX-1 pulled out of the show. Then he went back last night and stole it out of the hangar. Dad says he'll kill Ray when he catches him! This time he's not fooling, guys. That plane is his lifework."

She started to cry again. "You've got to help me!"

"That malfunction was real," Frank assured her. "Ray was just as scared as I was and just as confused about what had happened." He looked into her eyes. "Ray is my friend, and I trust him. We'll do everything we can to find out what happened. I'm sure there's an explanation. Ray's no thief."

Joe shot his older brother a warning glance. We have no guarantee about anything, it said. Better not get her hopes up.

"Whatever's going on," Joe said, "the first person for us to talk to is your dad."

"You won't be the first person *he's* talked to, though," Moira said, sniffling again. "Dad's already reported the theft to the Bayport Police, and he's called a press conference for ten this morning at the hangar!"

Frank, Joe, and Moira piled into the Hardys' van and headed for the airfield. The snow was falling more heavily. Bayport's streets were slick with new snow on top of old ice, so Frank drove cautiously. As they drove, Joe fiddled with the controls of the radio.

"What are you looking for?" Frank asked.

"News. Maybe they've already picked up on the story. We might hear something we don't know yet. Wait, here's something."

"The space shuttle *Discovery* made another perfect landing at Edwards Air Force Base, in California today," the announcer said. "The routine mission was completed in style, and the president was there to witness its descent."

"Turn it up louder, Joe," Frank said.

Joe turned the sound up, and the announcer continued, "The president, a former fighter pilot and director of NASA—the National Aeronautics and Space Administration—continues to show a lively interest in the space program and its goals."

"I heard about this," said Frank enthusiastically. "The president is going to ride the space shuttle."

Joe looked incredulous. "No way. They'd never let him take that big a risk."

"He's not really going into space, but they're going to let him experience what it's like. He's going to ride from California back to Florida in the shuttle."

"How would he do that?" Joe asked skeptically.

"They're going to mount the shuttle piggyback on a specially prepared 747," Frank explained. "The 747 takes off, flying low and slow all the way to Florida. The president, a couple of staff members, two astronauts, and a news crew will be on board the shuttle for the ride."

"We've got something more important to think about than the shuttle," Moira reminded them abruptly.

"We'll find Ray for you, Moira, don't worry," Frank insisted, frowning as he stared through the snow. "I'm sure he couldn't have gone far."

"Wow," Joe said as they entered the airfield's main gate to see the crowd of reporters around the grandstand, which was still in place. Max Lachlan was at his podium.

As Joe approached with Frank and Moira, he spotted Jill standing in front of the crowd of reporters, busily taking notes. Joe grinned at her, but she didn't even notice him.

"I felt triumphant," Lachlan was saying, "but today I am a defeated man. I was betrayed by a man I placed my trust in. He's stolen my masterpiece."

Joe noticed that Officer Con Reilly, standing beside Max Lachlan at the podium, looked uncomfortable. Con Reilly, a member of Bayport's police force, was well-known to the Hardys.

"Mr. Lachlan," Con interrupted, clearing his throat. "The worst thing a person can do in these circumstances is leap to conclusions. So far the evidence of a connection between the disappearance of your aircraft and its pilot is only circumstantial."

"Come now, officer." Lachlan's white hair was messed up, and he looked very upset. "The connection is obvious! Also, Ray Adamec was the only person other than Moira, my daughter, and myself, who knew the password to unarm our alarm system. He must have had this planned from the start! It's partly my fault for trusting him, but I didn't know until recently that he was dishonorably discharged from the navy only six months ago!"

Frank blinked in disbelief. As reporters called out questions, he turned to Moira. "Did you know about that?" he whispered.

Moira looked uncomfortable. "Of course," she snapped. "It was one of the first things Ray told me. His temper caused it. He got into an argument with a superior officer, and he punched him. But he told me my dad had known all about his discharge since the day he started work.''

Jill Stern spoke up then. ''Mr. Lachlan, do you have any idea where Adamec might have taken the MAX-1?''

Lachlan frowned, thinking. ''I'm afraid I don't, young lady. The only thing I know for certain is that he must have taken it in the dead of night, flying low to avoid radar detection. You see, the MAX-1's computer controls will allow you to fly at an altitude of a few feet for hours, no more visible to air radar than a car on the highway. He could have run along for miles just above ground level, and then zoomed straight up into the sky.''

He stared out at the reporters grimly. ''Our only hope is that he'll be spotted when he stops for fuel. The MAX-1 runs on regular automotive-grade gasoline. Such an unusual-looking vehicle should be noticed when it pulls up for gas.''

As Joe, Frank, and Moira listened to the questions and answers, Moira grew more and more upset. ''There's something wrong about all this,'' she said at last.

''What do you mean?'' asked Frank.

''I can't put my finger on it, but—''

Just then a television reporter asked, ''How does this setback affect your plans to market the MAX-1?'' Moira stopped to listen.

"I'm in a very bad position," Max Lachlan confessed. "All my development money was tied up in that one plane, and I don't know how I'll raise the money to build a second one."

"What?" Moira looked confused. Then her expression changed to one of anger. "That does it," she said.

"What does?"

She turned to Joe, her face red with indignation. "What about the MAX-2?" she demanded in a harsh whisper. "He acts as if it doesn't even exist, and it's all finished and ready for flight!"

Joe looked at Frank in surprise. "Why would your dad lie?" he asked Moira.

"I don't know." The girl's eyes narrowed. "He always overdramatizes things. This time he's gone too far. Ray's missing, and he didn't steal Dad's plane."

Her eyes flashed defiantly. "He may even be in danger because of the plane. And all my dad is doing is telling lies. Well, I'm going to put a stop to this!"

Chapter

5

"I NEED TO TALK TO HIM," Moira said, pushing through the crowd toward her father as the press conference ended and the reporters rushed off to file their stories. Joe and Frank followed Moira toward her father.

Max Lachlan was still answering questions for a few reporters. Finally, overwhelmed, he waved them all away and strode off with Con Riley.

"Dad!" When Moira finally reached him, he stopped and glared impatiently past her to Frank and Joe.

"What are *they* doing here?" he demanded gruffly.

"They're friends of mine and Ray's," Moira said. "They can help us."

"Friends of *his!*" Max Lachlan snorted. "The last thing we need is a couple of kids poking around in this. For all I know, they're in this with Adamec."

He grabbed Officer Reilly's shoulder and pointed at Frank. "This is the one who went up in the MAX-1 with Adamec yesterday," he said. "Ask him where his buddy took my aircraft."

Con Reilly gave Frank a sympathetic wink before trying to calm the angry aircraft designer. "We're going to follow up on every lead, Mr. Lachlan. But I don't think Fenton Hardy's sons are likely suspects. Their father's the best private investigator I've ever known, and his sons' reputations are, well . . ."

"Well, what?" demanded Lachlan.

"Well . . ." Reilly eyed the boys, then decided to placate Lachlan. "Maybe I'd better have you two in for questioning later," he said. "You, too, Miss Lachlan."

"Me?" Moira said, surprised. "But I'm his daughter! Dad, wait," she called to Lachlan as he stalked off. "We need to talk!"

"Meet me back here this evening," he shouted over his shoulder. "And don't bring those two with you when you come!" He disappeared into the hangar with two other police officers.

"Hmm," Joe said, watching him disappear. "What was that about a temper?"

"He's so pigheaded," Moira fumed, red-faced. "Sometimes I just want to clobber him!"

"Want help?" Frank said, only half joking. Lachlan's attempt to turn Con Reilly against them had stung.

Joe jammed his hands into his pockets and followed Frank and Moira back across the airfield toward the van. Something didn't seem right about the whole situation, he thought, passing the STOL hangar and glancing in at the enormous carrier. Why would Ray do something as stupid as steal the MAX-1? It would be a cinch to identify. Ray must have known he could never get away with it. And what would he do with such a machine? He couldn't fly it— and he couldn't sell it. No, it just didn't add up.

His eyes on Moira's and Frank's footprints in the thin layer of newly fallen snow, Joe tried to fit the pieces of the puzzle together.

When they reached the van, Moira turned to face Joe, her green eyes flashing. "Well, you're the expert detectives," she said, challenge in her voice. "I need to find Ray and prove that he's innocent. So what do we do now?"

Joe met her gaze and smiled slightly. He'd be glad to prove to Moira what good detectives he and Frank could be.

"We check out Ray's apartment, of course," he said to her. "I hope you have a key."

"No, but I know where he keeps his spare." She eyed Joe hopefully. "You think we might find some clues there?"

"Why not?" Joe climbed into the van. "Anything's worth a try."

Frank seemed lost in thought as they drove to Ray's apartment, on the other side of town. He was wondering how a guy as hard-working and ambitious as Ray Adamec could have been dishonorably discharged from the navy and told no one but his girlfriend. *And* stolen a multimillion-dollar aircraft and disappeared. He shook his head. It didn't sound anything like the Ray Adamec he had known. But then, the neighborhood they were driving through was more rundown than he'd expected. Ray's apartment turned out to be on the top floor of a ramshackle house on the edge of town.

"This is it?" Frank asked, parking the van at the curb. He sat, staring at the house's peeling paint and sagging front porch for a moment. "It's hard to believe."

"Appearances aren't everything," Moira said defensively as she got out of the van. "Ray doesn't care where he lives. All he's interested in is his work."

Frank thought about what she'd said as he followed behind her and Joe. Maybe Moira understood Ray in a way that Frank and Joe weren't able to.

Frank wished he could talk over his feelings about Ray with Callie, but she must have left for her winter vacation in Florida already. With all the goings-on that morning, Frank hadn't even said goodbye.

Moira stepped up on the wooden railing of the porch and reached up into a gutter. "Are you sure that can support your weight?" Joe asked. Moira pointedly ignored him.

"It's not there," she said. "Ray must have taken it."

"Not to worry," Joe said, leading the way up the stairs to the landing outside Ray's apartment. He pulled a set of lockpicks out of his coat pocket and eyed the lock on Ray's door. "I'll have us in in ten seconds. Start counting."

"Eight . . . nine . . ." Moira recited as Joe worked at the lock.

"Slow down," Joe grumbled, yanking on the lock.

"Nine and a half . . ."

Joe's hand jerked free of the lock and pick, and he stepped back to reveal the door swinging slowly open. He grinned at Moira and doffed an imaginary hat. "Ten," he said, and ushered her indoors.

"You really do know how to impress a girl," Frank whispered to Joe as he walked past him through the door.

Frank whistled when he saw the inside of the two-room apartment. It was a shambles. Clothes were strewn all over the floor. Every drawer was open. The desk and tabletop were covered with piles of paper. An old wing chair lay on its side, its upholstery shredded.

In the bedroom the scene was similar. Both sheets were ripped off the bed, and every drawer and closet was flung open and emptied.

"Somebody's ransacked this place!" Frank declared.

"No, they haven't." Moira's face turned pink. "It always looks like this. Ray isn't the neatest guy in the world."

"Looks okay to me," said Joe. "Let's check it out."

They examined the apartment carefully. Joe worked his way through the papers on the desk, hoping to find a clue as to Ray's whereabouts. Beneath a stack of file folders he found a looseleaf scrapbook. He opened it.

"Moira, are you sure Ray's one of the good guys?" he asked unhappily.

"What have you got?" Frank walked over to see, and Moira hurriedly joined them, peering over Frank's shoulder.

"It's full of newspaper clippings." Joe flipped through the pages. "About terrorist hijackings, bombings, murders, assassinations." He glanced at his brother. "Some of these look familiar," he muttered.

Frank nodded reluctantly. The implications made him very unhappy. "These are all Assassin activities," he answered. "Ray's been studying the Assassins."

"Are you sure he's only been studying them?" Joe persisted.

Moira stared at the notebook, confused. "What are you two talking about? What assassins?"

"The Assassins are a terrorist group," Frank told her. "A secret society determined to destabilize governments all over the world."

"And your boyfriend seems to know them pretty well," Joe added. He closed the scrapbook with a clap.

Moira took a step back, staring at the two brothers. "You can't possibly believe that Ray is one of these—these Assassins!" she protested.

Frank shook his head. "I don't know what to think anymore," he admitted.

"They're tricky," Joe added ominously. "You never know who could turn out to be one of them."

"Maybe even Frank or Joe Hardy!" said a voice from the doorway.

Joe whirled and saw a small bald-headed man standing in the doorway. It was the same man Jill had pointed out the day before—the man who had nearly run the Hardys over that night. This time he had a Colt .45 automatic in his right hand—and it was trained right at Joe.

"Get him!" shouted Joe, and Frank reacted

instantly, feinting to the right. When the man's attention, and his gun, turned to follow Frank, Joe hurled the scrapbook at his head.

Joe heard Moira scream as Frank leapt across the room, crashing hard into the gunman. The stranger was surprisingly quick, and he shifted his weight with the impact and threw Frank over his shoulder. Before Joe could move, the man had clipped Frank across the back with the butt of his gun.

The man turned back to face Joe and Moira, but this time he walked right into Joe's left hook.

It was a perfect punch. The man reeled back, stunned. "Hey, Frank!" Joe yelled as his brother sprang to his feet. "Get over here and help me!"

Frank did as he was told. With a swift karate kick, he knocked the man's gun from his hand. Joe stepped in, grabbed the man's wrist, spun him around, and slammed him into the wall. He kept the stranger's right arm twisted behind his back in a painful hammerlock.

"Okay, okay," the man said, grimacing. "Ease up. You got me!"

"Yeah," Frank said, panting. "But who've we got?"

"Commander Edgar Tracey! Naval Intelligence, working undercover!"

"Try again." Joe kept a tight hold on the

man while kicking the gun into the farthest corner of the room.

"It's true! Let me get out my ID and I'll prove it."

Joe exchanged a quick glance with his brother, then relaxed his grip and stepped back. "Okay," he said, "but move slowly. My brother gets nervous when he's been attacked. He might go for you."

Tracey straightened his jacket, looking annoyed. Then he reached into his pocket and produced his wallet. Frank examined the ID card. "Looks like the genuine article," he said.

"What are you doing here, Commander Tracey?" Joe asked angrily. "Why'd you try to run us over last night? Why the gun now?"

"I didn't try to run you over. You stepped out in front of my car!" the man protested. "As for the gun, you think I'd walk into a nest of suspected Assassins empty-handed?"

Joe gasped. "You thought *we* were Assassins?" he said.

"Both you and your friend Adamec. We've been watching him since his discharge. I suspected you might be his contacts. Once he disappeared, I figured you two might lead me to him."

"Well, your cover's blown now," Joe announced. "We're taking you in for a nice long conversation with a police friend of ours."

"I'm sorry," said Tracey, "but I can't do that."

He pivoted suddenly, driving his left elbow into Joe's temple. Stunned by the blow, Joe relaxed his grip, and Tracey broke free.

Frank started for the little man, but Tracey kicked out, catching him full in the chest. Frank's down jacket softened the full force of the blow, but he was still knocked backward a few feet. Before he could recover, the man had crashed through a closed window to the snow-covered ground two stories below.

The Hardys bolted for the window. Tracey landed like a cat and was almost to the door of the gray sedan.

"Too late," Frank said, watching the car screech off down the road. "He's gone!"

Chapter

6

"SOME VACATION," Joe said to himself as he stood at the kitchen counter, opening bags of take-out hamburgers, fries, and jumbo shakes. "I spend my mornings in the freezing snow. I watch my brother nearly get killed in a plane crash. I practically get run over by a bald man. The only cute, available girl I've seen all week disappears to write a story, and I'm stuck trying to help Moira find some guy she likes better than me."

He set plates of food down in front of Moira and Frank. "Some guys have all the luck," he concluded.

"Huh?" Frank asked.

Joe didn't even bother complaining directly

to his brother. Frank was deep into their mystery now and was determined to solve it. "Let's start at the beginning," he said to Moira, his mouth filled with french fries. He swallowed before continuing. "First, we're missing a plane and a pilot. Where are they, and are they together? And if they are together, did Ray actually steal the MAX-1?"

"That's what the evidence points to," Joe said. He slurped his thick shake.

"But it's all circumstantial!" Moira protested.

"Absolutely," Frank said. "So, did Ray really steal the MAX-1, and if so—why? I find it hard to believe Ray's an Assassin."

"But there's evidence that points to the contrary," Joe insisted. "Say he is an Assassin who's stolen the MAX-1. Where's he gone, and what's he going to do with the plane?" He turned to Moira. "What exactly did your father design it for?"

Moira's eyes widened. "Plenty of things, I guess. It's incredibly maneuverable. It could be used as a family vehicle, as Ray said. Or for low-level observation. Or as a fighter jet—"

"Wait." Joe wiped his mouth with a napkin. "A what?"

"A fighter jet—" Moira stopped and turned pink. "Oh, you don't think— The Max-1 isn't armed!"

"Okay, okay." Frank put a hand out to calm

them both. "So that's another question—whether the stolen vehicle could be used as a weapon. What I want to know, though, is why he said there's only one plane when he knows there's a second one ready to fly?"

Moira tossed her head impatiently. "Who knows?" she said. "As I said, Dad likes to be dramatic. If it's a choice between the truth and a good story, you can guess which he'll choose."

"Even when it's this serious?" Frank shook his head. "Hard to believe. What about investors, backers? Who financed the MAX-1, anyway? Could he have been trying to get them to fork up extra money?"

A look of surprise crossed Moira's face. "You know, I never asked him who backed the MAX project."

"We have a lot of questions for your father," Frank said. "For instance, I wonder if he knows the mysterious Edgar Tracey."

"Everyone finished eating?" Joe asked abruptly. "Then let's go have that talk with Moira's dad—whether he wants to or not!"

Even Joe cheered up as they stepped out of the Hardys' house. It was a beautiful late winter afternoon. The sun had just begun to set. The temperature had dropped, and the snow was falling in large, wet flakes. The paper boy had to walk with his bag of papers instead of riding his bike. Down the block a group of kids was building a snowman.

"Makes you wish you were a kid again, doesn't it?" said seventeen-year-old Joe, zipping his jacket. "Nothing to do all day but eat and play."

"Look." Frank nudged him and nodded toward their van, parked in the driveway. A man with a crew cut, in sunglasses, a navy blue parka, and red sneakers that were already wet-looking, was just darting around the front of the van.

"Hey!" Frank shouted. "What are you doing to our van!"

The man took off instantly. In a single movement Joe and Frank pounded after him. Frank's heart crashed in his chest as he pumped his legs, putting everything he could into the chase. Was this guy doing something to their van, like planting a bug in it? Or something worse?

Frank pushed on, even when he sensed that Joe had fallen a step or two behind. Though Joe was the stronger of the two, Frank had more stamina and made a better runner. It looked as if he'd need it because the man in the parka had rounded a corner half a block ahead.

"Hey!" Frank yelled between gasps for air. He turned the corner after the man, just in time to see him vault into a navy blue jeep. The driver, who turned to stare at Frank, was another man in a crew cut, wearing sunglasses and a parka. For a moment Frank thought he was seeing double.

The sight was enough to make him hesitate for an instant—long enough for Joe to catch up. "What's going on?" Joe demanded, panting for breath.

Frank didn't take the time to answer. The man they'd been chasing turned and pointed a .357 magnum at the Hardys out his window. The stranger squeezed off a shot that was muffled by the falling snow. Joe and Frank hit the ground and rolled for cover into a snowbank.

The driver threw the Jeep into gear, and it roared off down the street.

"Did you get the number?" Frank asked his brother.

"Nope—too much snow, but it was from Utah. Let's get back to the van."

Moira was waiting for them at the foot of their driveway. "Did I hear a shot?" she cried.

"No time to explain!" Joe gasped, reaching for the door of the van.

"Wait!" Frank yelled.

Joe froze.

Frank moved toward Joe very calmly and quietly. "Don't open that door," he said in a steady voice.

Joe immediately caught on. "You think they want us to chase them?"

Frank nodded.

"And when we open the door—boom."

Frank nodded again. "Let's check it out slowly and very carefully," Frank said.

Frank knew that any bomb can be found and neutralized. All it took was patience. "You check under the chassis," he said to Joe. "Don't forget the wheel wells. I'll take care of the body."

Frank ran a finger along every seam. He checked under the bumpers, anywhere a bomb could be hidden. At last he worked his way up to the front of the van.

Peering in through the driver's side window, Frank spotted it. A thin, almost invisible wire ran from under the driver's seat to the inside handle of the passenger door.

"Got it," he called to Joe and Moira. They joined him, and he pointed out the wire to them.

"What do we do?" asked Moira.

"Back off," said Frank. "I'll deal with it."

Moira looked doubtful but did as she was told. Frank knew everything about explosives, Joe assured her.

With Joe and Moira at a safe distance, Frank opened the driver's door gingerly. He followed the wire and felt under the driver's seat. Despite the frigid air, sweat was running down his forehead.

Then his fingers found something. He reached into his pocket and pulled out a small nail clipper. Reaching under the seat, he cautiously snipped a wire.

No explosion. Frank let out a sigh of relief.

Moments later they all stood beside the van, studying the device in Frank's hand. It was a small, round packet of plastic explosives. A trip detonator had been set to blow when the passenger door opened.

"Somebody doesn't like us," Joe said grimly.

"I'll say," Moira said. "Does this kind of thing happen to you guys often?"

"More than we'd like," Frank admitted.

Joe cleared his throat. "I hate to say it," he began, "but do you think this might have something to do with Ray?"

"Maybe." Frank looked down at the bomb. This time he noticed a second, smaller detonator on it. This one had a tiny antenna.

"What's this?" he muttered.

Joe followed his gaze. "Wow."

Frank was already thinking. "If someone wanted us gone that badly," he said, "they'd probably wait around somewhere and listen for the explosion. If they didn't hear it, they'd assume we'd disconnected the bomb—"

"And that's why they'd have a radio-controlled backup!" Joe pulled Moira away from the van with him. "Throw it, Frank!"

Frank looked around wildly. "Where?"

They were in the middle of a residential street

with little kids building a snowman at one end and a paper boy trudging along nearby with his bag of papers.

Frank was standing in the driveway with half a pound of high explosives in his hand.

He heard a tiny click inside the bomb's mechanism.

The look he shot his brother was one of sheer horror.

They were out of time!

Chapter

7

"MOVE! Get out of here!" Frank Hardy shouted at his brother and Moira.

They moved, dashing back toward the garage and house.

Frank looked around quickly. He had maybe three seconds—if he was lucky. Down the street he saw the kids with their snowman. In the other direction he saw the paper boy. Across the street . . .

Frank's arm flashed forward, and the explosive device sailed through the air like a football, its arc carrying it over a passing car. It landed just in front of the far curb, hit a patch of ice, and slid—right down into the storm drain Frank had targeted!

The explosion shook the entire block. Frank watched from behind the van, his hands covering his ears. The force of the explosion blew a manhole cover two yards into the air, toppled the snowman, and even broke one window. Other than those effects, however, the explosion caused no harm.

"That was the greatest throw I've ever seen!" Joe had appeared at his brother's side and was pounding Frank's back. "I was really worried for a minute there. What would I have told Mom and Dad if you hadn't thrown it?"

Frank laughed a little shakily.

Moira came over and hugged them both, hard, tears of relief in her eyes.

It took over an hour before the Hardy brothers and Moira had finished giving Con Reilly and two other uniformed police officers their reports.

"You say this jeep had Utah plates?" Reilly repeated. "Did you get a number "

"No, but how many jeeps with Utah plates could there be in Bayport?" Frank asked.

Con Reilly shook his head. "I don't get it, boys. Why would these fellows travel all the way from Utah to blow up your van?"

"I don't know," said Joe. "I tell you, Con, I'd never seen those guys before, but there was something familiar about them."

"Then you'd better think harder and try to remember where you've seen them," said Reilly. "It's obvious to me that you've stirred up a hornets' nest. What have you learned lately that might make someone nervous enough to try to blow you up?"

Joe started to answer, when he noticed a small hatchback pull up to the curb behind Reilly. Out popped Jill Stern, Moira's reporter friend. Instantly Joe's face brightened, and he forgot whatever he'd been about to say to Con.

"Jill!" He waved her over. "What are you doing here?"

"I heard about the bombing." Jill joined them quickly, glancing from the boys to Officer Reilly. "I have a police-band radio in the car," she explained. "Is Moira here?"

"Here I am." Moira rushed over from where she'd been talking with another officer. The two girls hugged each other before Jill looked her friend over carefully.

"Moira, are you okay?"

"Sure," Moira said lightly. "Thanks to Frank and Joe."

Both girls focused on Joe Hardy, and he felt his face turning red. "So you're a hero again," Jill said jokingly.

"Uh, not really. Frank did it. I was back by the garage." Joe could have kicked himself for sounding so dimwitted.

"Well, hero or not, I've got a million questions," Jill declared. "I can't believe I'm the first reporter here!"

"I'm afraid you'll have to wait, young lady," Con Reilly said firmly despite his pleasant smile. "Joe was just about to tell me something important."

"Oh, yeah." Joe lowered his voice. "We met a man named Edgar Tracey who said he was with Naval Intelligence. You know anything about him?"

Reilly's expression was thoughtful. "Where'd you meet him?" he asked.

"At Ray Adamec's apartment," said Frank. "He said he'd been watching Ray since he was discharged."

"I'll put a call in to Naval Intelligence when I get back to the station." Reilly frowned. "Maybe they can tell us more about your friend Ray as well."

"If Tracey does turn out to be legit," said Joe, "tell them he's a lousy driver. He almost ran us over last night!"

"Are you talking about the man from the restaurant?" Jill asked, having eavesdropped on their conversation. "I think I got a picture of him on the roll of film from the MAX-1 demonstration yesterday morning."

Reilly perked up immediately. "I'd like to see it," he said to Jill.

"Sure. If you'll fill me in on the Adamec case."

Reilly grimaced but then relented. He turned to the Hardys. "I'm going to head back to the station with this very curious young lady and see what she has. I know it's pointless to ask you two to stay out of this. But, please, call me before you do anything foolish."

Joe was all innocence as he replied, "If I plan anything foolish, I'll remember to call."

Jill and Moira laughed as Reilly followed Jill to her car.

"Now what?" Moira asked as the cars pulled away.

Joe, who was staring after Jill's hatchback, failed to answer.

"Well, we were on our way to talk to your dad before we were so rudely interrupted," Frank said. "So let's go talk to him."

By the time they arrived at the airfield, it was dark. The snow had stopped falling. It was a chilly, clear night, and the hard-packed snow crunched underfoot as they entered through the unguarded gate.

"He's not going to like this," Moira warned. "He's got you guys linked with Ray in his mind."

"Frankly, Moira, I don't care anymore," Joe

said. "Something big is going on, and I think your dad knows more than he's saying."

He reached for the doorknob. It turned easily, and he pushed the door open.

Facing him, not more than a yard away, was the man in the navy blue parka. For an instant he and Joe stared at each other, unmoving. The man's hand was outstretched, reaching for the doorknob. He'd been ready to turn it when Joe pushed the door open. Behind him stood his twin—also in shock.

In the next instant the man slammed the door closed in Joe's face. Joe and Frank recovered from the surprise of seeing their attackers up close and rushed inside.

Max Lachlan's workspace was as chaotic as Ray Adamec's apartment, but on a much larger scale. There were cartons and packing crates everywhere. Piles of machinery littered the floor, some covered with tarpaulins. Engines hummed and lights blinked on and off, as if Lachlan had an experiment in progress.

"There they go!" yelled Frank.

Joe caught a glimpse of the two men before they darted behind a huge wooden packing crate fifteen yards away. Joe gave chase first, followed by Frank. Joe followed the flash of red sneakers. The two men split up, and Joe and Frank split up as well, Joe continuing to track the red shoes.

"What about my dad?" Moira cried.

"Check if he's all right!" Frank tossed the words over his shoulder.

Moira dashed to the back of the hangar and up a flight of rickety stairs to her father's office, an enclosed loft in the hangar's far right-hand corner.

As Frank rounded a pile of packing crates, his quarry leapt out, catching him with a knee in the gut. Then he followed that up with a chop to the back of Frank's neck.

Frank grunted and stumbled, falling on one knee. But he kicked out, caught his opponent's leg, and brought him down as well. The two landed in a heap, punching and grappling.

Just as Joe had almost caught up with the man he was chasing, the man wheeled around to face him with the .357 magnum drawn. Before he could pull the trigger, Joe took a great leap, crashing into the smaller man with a flying dropkick.

The man reeled backward and dropped his gun, which went skittering across the cement floor. When he moved toward Joe again, he was brandishing a four-foot piece of pipe. He swung the pipe like a baseball bat. Joe dodged each blow successfully.

Meanwhile, Frank and his opponent had gotten to their feet, each waiting for the other to make the first move. Just then all four fighters were frozen in their tracks by Moira's cry from her father's office.

"Frank! Joe! Help!"

Frank and Joe hesitated for just a second to look up at the loft. A second was all the men in parkas needed to escape.

"Come quickly! I think my dad's having a heart attack!"

Chapter

8

"HELP HIM, PLEASE!" Moira cried.

As the two attackers made their way out the door, Frank and Joe bounded up the stairs to Max Lachlan's office.

"Oh, no." Frank stared at the room. The office was a mess. Furniture was strewn everywhere. Obviously a struggle had taken place. Max Lachlan lay on the floor, cradled in his daughter's arms. His face was blue, and his hands clutched his chest as he gasped desperately.

Moira looked stricken as she glanced up at them.

"Move over." Frank dropped down beside Moira and immediately began administering CPR. Joe grabbed the phone to dial 911 but set it down immediately. The phone was dead. He checked the cord. It had been yanked from the wall.

"Phone's no good," he told his brother.

"That's okay. We'll use the one in the van and take him to the hospital ourselves. We can call ahead to get them ready for us. It's faster than with an ambulance."

The three young people struggled to get Lachlan to his feet. He was a big, heavy man, and he was in no condition to help them. He groaned faintly.

Between them the brothers muscled Lachlan as gently as they could out of the office and to the landing. At the top of the stairs Joe grabbed his legs and Frank caught him under the armpits. Then they carefully maneuvered him down the narrow staircase.

"Give me your keys," Moira demanded of Frank. She took the keys and dashed across the big floor of the hangar. She hit a button, and the giant bay doors opened. She ran through them and reappeared a moment later, driving the brothers' van right inside.

The Hardys laid Lachlan down on the floor of the van as gently as possible. Joe and Moira stayed in back to tend to him, while Frank jumped into the driver's seat and took off.

"Bayport Hospital isn't far from here," Frank

said, grabbing the cellular phone. "I'll let them know we're coming."

"Who were those men?" Moira demanded furiously, looking down at her unconscious father. "What did they want with him?"

Frank made his call, and then switched off the phone. "The hospital's ready," he told Moira. "I'm sure your father will tell us everything once he's recovered."

Joe wasn't so sure. *If* he recovers, he thought.

"Miss Lachlan?" The doctor approached Moira, Frank, and Joe in the brightly lit emergency waiting room. Moira looked up expectantly. They'd been waiting for what felt like hours, and her face showed the strain of worry and exhaustion.

"Your father's resting comfortably, and we've moved him up to the coronary care unit," the doctor said. "We gave him a sedative, so he's very groggy."

Moira took a deep breath and tried to relax. "It was a heart attack, then?" she asked.

"We think so. But there are some . . . irregularities. We have to run some tests. Then he'll need several days at least in recovery."

"But he'll be okay?"

"Yes," the doctor assured her with an understanding smile. "His chances are very good."

As the doctor left, Moira sighed with relief

and leaned against Joe. He looked at her, surprised. Then he reminded himself that Moira was someone else's girlfriend. Still, he did put an arm around her to comfort her. "Don't worry," he said. "It'll work out okay."

Frank had put a call in to Con Reilly as soon as they got to the emergency room. When he arrived, he approached the little group, looking frazzled and sleepy.

"Don't you boys ever rest?" he asked. "My wife doesn't appreciate my charging out of the house at"—he peered blearily at his watch—"eleven-thirty on a Sunday night. Believe me, Frank and Joe Hardy don't win any popularity contests with Mrs. Con Reilly."

"It's important, Con," said Frank.

The officer sighed and nodded. "Would I be here if it wasn't? Can we talk to the patient?"

The young doctor was reluctant to let them speak with Lachlan. "He needs his rest," he insisted stubbornly. "He's not a healthy man, and he's been through a lot. In any case, he's too groggy to make much sense."

"Sorry, Doc. I know it's a bad idea," Officer Reilly said, "but believe me, he'd want to talk to us. He'd insist on it."

Finally the doctor relented, and Reilly, Frank, Joe, and Moira went up to the patient's room and gathered around his bed. Moira gasped at the sight of her father lying half asleep, with half a dozen tubes leading into and out of him.

The doctor was right, Joe decided. Max Lachlan did not look healthy. He was a far cry from the big, strapping man they'd seen that morning. It was scary how quickly a person could age.

Lachlan eyed Frank and Joe suspiciously from his bed. "What are they doing here?" he mumbled through his tubes.

"Frank and Joe saved your life, Dad," Moira said, trying to keep the exasperation out of her voice.

Her father grunted, unimpressed. "Sure—after their friends tried to kill me."

"What makes you think those creeps were our friends?" Frank protested. "They tried to kill us before they went after you!"

"Yeah, sure. You're all in this together. You two, Adamec, those thugs—all of you." He sounded as if he had cotton balls in his mouth, but he was making sense.

"I don't think that's the case, Mr. Lachlan," Con Reilly said to the patient. "If you could tell us what happened, we'd appreciate it."

"Dad, you can trust Joe and Frank," Moira insisted. "They're on our side. They were the ones who brought you here."

Lachlan closed his eyes and seemed to doze off. After a moment he said, "All right. I was going over some blueprints when I heard a noise. I went to the door, and some goon stuck his gun in my face.''

"What goon?" asked Reilly. "What did he look like?"

"I don't know." Lachlan turned his head away, exhausted. "Medium height. Crew cut. Navy blue parka, and red tennis shoes. He wore sunglasses, so I couldn't see his eyes."

"What did he want?"

Lachlan sighed. "Adamec. I said I didn't know where he was. They didn't believe me. They started busting things up. Threatening to kill me.''

"Then what happened?" Reilly demanded.

"I started feeling shooting pains up my left arm. I heard a car pull up. It must have been Moira and these boys. The next thing I knew I was on the floor and I couldn't breathe." He opened his eyes again. "That's all I can remember.''

"Okay," Reilly said.

At that moment the door swung open and a pair of hospital orderlies in white uniforms, surgical masks, and rubber gloves rolled a gurney into the room.

"Time for tests," one of them announced loudly, moving toward the bed and beginning to unhook Lachlan's tubes.

"We're not finished here," Reilly protested.

"This won't take long." The orderlies quickly transferred Lachlan to the gurney. "We'll have him back before you know it."

Before anyone could object further, the orderlies wheeled the patient out the door.

As they slipped the gurney out the door, Frank glanced after them, wondering why they were wearing surgical masks. His gaze fell to one orderly's shoes—and froze.

The man was wearing red sneakers.

"Hey!" Frank yelled, springing for the door.

The orderly spun around, held up his hand and sprayed something into Frank's face from a tiny canister.

Mace! Frank reeled back, covering his eyes. The orderly shoved him back against his brother and Reilly, then slammed the door on all of them.

"The sneakers!" Frank cried, rubbing frantically at his stinging eyes.

"Here," said Moira. "Try this." She handed Frank a pitcher of water. As he splashed it into his eyes, Joe and Con Reilly raced to the door. It was jammed. Reilly backed off three paces, then drove his shoulder into the door. It gave way with a loud crack.

Joe and Con Reilly dashed out into the hallway, with Moira right behind them. Frank, dabbing at his eyes with the edge of his sweatshirt, brought up the rear.

Joe caught a flash of red as an orderly rounded a distant corner. "Come on!" he shouted.

The Hardys, Moira, and Con shot around the corner just seconds after the kidnappers—but they still were too late. At the end of the hallway was an elevator, and its doors were sliding closed.

The two hoods were inside, with Max Lachlan strapped to the gurney.

Chapter

9

"JOE, FRANK, you've got to stop them!" Moira cried.

"We'll try!" Joe shouted, and grabbed the arm of a passing nurse. "Where's the nearest staircase?" he demanded.

The nurse pointed down the hall. "Come on!" Joe sprinted for the door.

They all tore down the flights of stairs with Joe in the lead. "We'll catch them," Joe muttered to himself, his feet flying over four steps at a time.

The young people quickly outdistanced Officer Reilly, and halfway down he was forced to pause on a landing to catch his breath. "Con!" Frank called back over his shoulder. "You okay?"

"Go on without me." Reilly clutched his side, breathing shallowly. "I'll catch up, don't worry."

Joe burst out of the stairwell on the first floor, followed by Frank and Moira. "Which way?" Joe cried.

"This way!" Frank chose, pointing toward the emergency entrance. Joe took his advice and burst outside—just in time to see the rear door of an ambulance being pulled closed by the guy in red sneakers. The white and blue van roared out of the parking lot, its tires squealing.

"That's them!" Joe shouted. He ran to their van and gunned the engine to life as Frank and Moira leapt in. They roared off in flying pursuit of the speeding ambulance.

"You see it?" Moira asked, leaning forward from the backseat to peer through the windshield at Bayport's deserted nighttime streets.

"There it is," Joe said grimly, catching a glimpse of the white and blue vehicle careening around a corner a few blocks ahead. He pushed hard on the accelerator, closing the distance a little as the ambulance hesitated at a number of intersections, started to turn right on one street, then went straight instead and turned left on the next.

"These guys aren't locals," Joe muttered. "They don't know where they're going!"

"Good," snapped Frank. "That means we have the advantage."

Joe pushed the accelerator harder as they pursued the ambulance up a highway on-ramp. "Watch out for icy patches," Frank said sharply.

"Forget the ice," Moira snapped. "Just catch those kidnappers."

Once on the highway, Joe pushed the accelerator to the floor, and the van's turbo engine surged forward with extra power. They were gaining on the ambulance. It was obvious that it wasn't nearly as powerful as their van.

Just then the flashing light on the ambulance's roof was turned on and its siren wailed.

"What're they doing?" Moira asked, surprised.

Frank shook his head. "It's like they're trying to make this easy for us."

"Fine with me," Joe said, and closed the gap a little more.

A moment later Frank glanced into the sideview mirror and turned pale. "Uh-oh. Now I get it."

Joe, raising his eyes to the rearview mirror, said, "Oh, no! Not a cop!"

"They put us right where they wanted us," Frank admitted with a groan. "No cop will stop a speeding ambulance. But we're dead ducks."

"What do we do?" Joe demanded.

Frank's face turned grim. "Keep going!" he told him. "We'll explain it to the officers *after* we catch up to that ambulance!"

Sweat popped out on Joe's forehead as he obeyed orders, ignoring the wail of the police siren. The Hardys' van was fast, but the police car was faster. It pulled up beside the van, and the officer waved angrily for Joe to pull over.

"What do I do now?" Joe said.

"Keep going," Moira ordered through gritted teeth.

When Joe obeyed, the police car began to crowd him, and nudged him off to the side of the road. The cruiser's right front bumper edged ahead of their van and veered in to the right. "Hey!" Joe yelled, swerving to avoid a collision.

The van clipped the edge of a snowbank, throwing up an arc of slush and ice and forcing Joe to fight to control the wheel.

"This is no good, Moira!" he gasped. "We've got to pull over."

"You're right," Frank admitted. "We've lost them for now."

Joe slowed the van to a stop. The police car pulled in ahead, cutting him off.

"Out of the van, kid!" The burly, red-faced patrolman was at Joe's window in an instant, his .38 drawn.

"How're we going to explain this?" Frank muttered under his breath to Joe as two more police cars skidded up behind the van. Then he breathed a sigh of relief—out of the cruiser climbed Con Reilly.

"Come on, Reilly, it's so late." Frank brandished his wristwatch wearily. "Can't we finish the report in the morning? This has been a busy day for us.''

He glanced over at his younger brother. Joe rolled his eyes at Frank's understatement. Busy day? They'd had guns pointed at them, one of which had been fired. They'd narrowly escaped being blown to bits. They'd been in two fights and a high-speed chase over icy roads. They were exhausted, and all Joe could think of was his bed.

''Sorry, boys, but we're doing this one by the book. I need your statement, and I'm taking it now,'' Con Reilly replied, stifling a yawn. ''Even if it takes till dawn.''

Joe hated it when Reilly got like that. Usually, when he and Frank were working on a case, he was a good ally. But sometimes when he decided things had gotten out of hand, he clicked into ''official'' mode and began doing everything by the numbers. It was clear that was how he was going to run the Ray Adamec investigation.

''One more time,'' Reilly said. ''I need a motive for Adamec's disappearance.''

Moira had patiently sat answering questions for the past hour, but now her composure gave way to anger. ''How many different ways are you going to ask the same question?'' she exploded. ''My father and my fiancé have obviously both been kidnapped by two men, whom you should be out catching!''

"Whoa, steady there, miss. We have an all-points bulletin out for those guys, but there are lots of questions to sort out yet."

Moira stood up abruptly. "Well, you're going to have to sort them out without me. I've had enough, and I'm leaving." She turned to Joe and Frank. "Are you coming with me?"

Frank cocked one eyebrow at Reilly. "We really are exhausted, Con. Why don't you let us go home and catch a few hours of shut-eye?"

Reilly considered. "Okay," he said finally. "You win. I'll see you at nine. But stay out of trouble till then!"

It was bitterly cold outside the Bayport police station as Joe, Frank, and Moira walked toward the van. The snow squeaked under their feet, and their breath froze in white puffs in front of them.

"Can we take you home, Moira?" Frank asked. "Your car is still in front of our house, but we can ask Con to pick you up in the morning."

"No." The pretty, brown-haired girl gazed out the window. "I can't sleep yet." She thought for a minute, then asked, "Can you take me back to the hangar?"

"Why now?" Joe asked, incredulous.

Moira frowned at him. "You're supposed to be the detective. Maybe those two guys dropped something that could identify them. Maybe there's a clue in my dad's papers. Maybe I just want to clean up the mess!"

"Okay, you're right," Frank said, calming her. He thought about Ray's temper, and Max's temper. If ever three people were well-matched, it was these three. In a real three-way argument, he decided, he'd put his money on the dark-haired girl, though.

Joe slid down in his seat. "Wake me up when we get there," he said.

Joe dreamed a wild mishmash of images. There was the MAX-1, soaring through the sky and then almost crashing. There were the faces of Max and Ray, distorted with fury, yelling at each other. Guns were everywhere, and Edgar Tracey kept slipping in and out of windows. And throughout the dream, over and over again, flashed the images of the two crew-cut attackers. They leered, they glared—somehow Joe knew he'd seen them before. But where?

Joe felt his shoulder being gently shaken. "Okay, partner, we're here," his older brother was saying.

Joe opened his eyes and saw that they were parked in front of Lachlan's hangar. It was deep night. Across the runway the enormous STOL transport of International Expeditors warmed its engines, ready to take off now that the weekend airshow was over.

Joe blinked, still groggy with sleep. "It's leaving *now?*" he said, bewildered. "In the middle of the night?"

"Maybe they've got another show tomorrow morning," Frank suggested.

Shaking his head, Joe stumbled out of the van and followed Frank and Moira to the hangar.

Something clicked into place in Joe's mind and he stopped dead, staring at the big STOL as it began to taxi slowly.

"Wait a second!" he shouted. He plunged his gloved hand deep into the pocket of his jacket and pulled the crumpled International Expeditors' brochure out of his pocket.

"What is it? What've you got?" Frank demanded.

Joe opened the brochure, turning the pages, until he came to one he'd briefly glanced at the morning before. On the page was a photograph of the STOL with a half-dozen men in coveralls standing in front of it.

Joe showed the photograph to Frank and Moira. The caption identified them as "International Expeditors' top-notch engineering staff." In the front row, grinning out at the camera, were the two men with crew cuts who had kidnapped Max Lachlan!

"That's it!" Joe shouted. "That's where I'd seen those guys before!"

Frank pointed at the big STOL taxiing down

the runway. "And that's where they are, along with a Jeep, an ambulance, and Max Lachlan!"

"And maybe Ray and the MAX-1 as well!" Moira exclaimed. The two brothers stared at her, realizing she was probably right. In one movement the three of them began to run flat out toward the carrier.

Frank didn't know what he'd do if they caught up with the giant aircraft. He didn't have time to think about it. He just ran. The STOL made a slow turn at the end of the runway and prepared for take-off. Frank slowed to a standstill, staring at the windows along the side. He caught a glimpse of movement in one of them.

There in the window was one of their tormentors. He spotted Frank, grinned, and waved!

Then the big plane rose effortlessly into the darkened sky. Frank, Joe, and Moira stood rooted to the ground, helpless and frustrated, watching it fly away.

Chapter

10

"OKAY, FOLKS, let's take it from the top," Frank Hardy said. Joe settled into his father's easy chair, willing to let his big brother run the show.

It must have been nearly four in the morning by the time they had called the police about the STOL's departure, Joe reflected. Con Reilly had still been at the station. When they told him about their discovery, he'd immediately called the Federal Aviation Administration.

But the STOL transport proved to be untrackable. Just our luck, Joe thought, gazing out the window at the falling snow. It must have been flying too low to be tracked by radar, or it was sending out a false identification signal. It was confirmed that the STOL had taken off without clearance and that its crew had filed no flight plan.

Finally the Hardys and Moira had given up and driven home. The boys gave Moira their aunt Gertrude's room to sleep in and sacked out themselves for a few hours.

Now, at nine o'clock sharp, they all were assembled in the living room: Frank, Joe, Moira, Con Reilly, and Jill Stern, who had traded her photos for access to this meeting.

Fine with me, thought Joe wearily as he reached for one of the doughnuts Con Reilly had brought. Moira could use a friend right now.

"First, the cast of characters," Frank was saying. "There's Ray Adamec, the test pilot. There's Max Lachlan, the inventor. We've got a man who calls himself Edgar Tracey and claims to be with Naval Intelligence. Finally there are our two friends from International Expeditors. We've also got two new aircraft, the MAX-1 and the STOL transport. Con, what do you have?"

Joe smiled to himself. He knew Con Reilly considered himself a crack investigator and that it sometimes grated on his nerves to have to share information with two teenage sleuths. But time and again the boys had proved that it was better to work with the Hardys than against them.

The police officer wiped red jam off his lips with a napkin. He stood up and wearily opened a file folder.

"Well, let's start with Adamec," he said in a resigned voice. "He's twenty-four now?" Moira nodded.

"You met him when he was an Explorer advising your scout troop, right, Frank?"

Frank nodded, and Reilly continued. "He went to NROTC in college, then right to flight school in Pensacola. After that he spent almost a year flying an F-14 Tomcat fighter off the carrier *Forrestal*. By all reports he was a real top gun, a great pilot, but he had a big temper and got into an argument with a superior. The details are sketchy, but it looks like he took a poke at an officer. He was given a dishonorable discharge."

"We know all that," Frank said impatiently. "What else?"

"Apparently, he'd started writing to Max Lachlan while he was still in the navy, telling him how much he admired his work. When Lachlan heard that Ray was out of the navy, he offered him a job, and Ray came back to Bayport."

Reilly closed the file and sat down, reaching for another doughnut. Frank thought for a moment. "You think he set it up so he could get close to Max?" he asked, glancing at Moira to see how she was taking all this.

"Anything's possible, but I have the impression Adamec is a real straight arrow."

"What about the Assassin connection?" asked Joe. "Have you found anything to indicate that Ray is one of them?"

Reilly shook his head. "Just that scrapbook we found in his apartment. Maybe he is an Assassin. Or maybe he's just curious about them."

"Okay, let's go on," Frank suggested.

"Now for Max Lachlan," said Reilly. "That is if you don't mind, Moira?"

Moira told him to go ahead and said she was sorry she didn't know much about her father's business, but she'd been away at school and he'd never shared much about it with her.

"Max has lived in Bayport all his life," Reilly continued, "except for four years at MIT, a couple of years in the air force in the early sixties, and a stint in the engineering department at General Dynamics right after that. Married Moira's mother, Ellen, his high-school sweetheart, around that time. Moira was born two years later. Wife died thirteen years after that."

Joe glanced over at Moira. She had a sad

expression on her face, but she was sitting straight-backed and alert, intent on business.

"My mom and dad were both testing a new plane, an early MAX-1 prototype," Moira explained in a low voice. "It crashed. My dad was in the hospital for weeks afterward. He didn't even know she had died until ten days later. He's never flown a plane since then."

There was a short silence. Jill patted Moira's hand. Then Frank cleared his throat uncomfortably. "I looked through some old newspaper stories on the computer this morning before you guys got up," he confessed. "You know, about his getting bumped off the space shuttle project. Looks to me like it was all political. He'd rubbed a few people the wrong way. Turns out he was right about the design of the tiles on the shuttle's outer skin. But he'd invested his own money in his design, and when it was rejected, he was in deep financial trouble. It must have taken him years to get the money for the MAX-1."

"How'd he raise the money for the MAX project?" Joe wanted to know.

"That's what I've been researching," Jill said. Moira looked surprised. "Your dad never answered that question when I asked it," Jill said defensively. "So I did some research. I went through everything—even his bank records."

She glanced at Moira apologetically. "Whoever was bankrolling Max, he or she hid it well."

"What about International Expeditors?" asked Joe. "Their brochure claimed that Max designed their STOL."

Frank shook his head. "I tried to find out about them on the computer. Nothing. No records. Zero. Couldn't find a thing."

"What about the address on their brochure?" asked Moira.

"It's a dummy," Frank said. "That address is a truck stop in the middle of the Utah desert, a hundred miles from nowhere."

At the word *Utah*, Joe's and Moira's eyes widened. "Wait a minute," Joe said, putting down his doughnut.

"That's where the jeep was from!" said Moira.

Frank stared at them, open-mouthed. "How could I have forgotten?" he said. "How dumb! I didn't even think—"

"You're tired, Frank," Joe said sympathetically. "Two hours' sleep in two days, right?"

"So wait," Jill said, her mind working fast. "Say that after Moira's mother died, International Expeditors approached Max with a deal. He was flat broke, right?"

"Right," said Frank eagerly, leaning forward. "So of course he was happy to design a plane for them—the STOL. They paid him enough to repay his debts and start work on his MAX project. Maybe they even gave him cash to pay for that one, too. The only catch could have been that he'd have to hide the money.''

"He couldn't have been particular about who he dealt with," Joe agreed. "He probably made the bargain and hoped for the best.''

Frank picked up the story, his eyes bright. "But when the MAX-1 and Ray disappeared, he got worried. He knew the MAX-1 could be a dangerous high-technology weapon in the wrong hands. So he kept quiet about the second MAX, in case the same people tried to steal that, too!''

"So you think those 'people' might have been Assassins?" Joe asked quietly. "And Ray's one of them?''

Frank hesitated. "I hope not," he said. "But it sure looks like he was in the wrong place at the right time." He frowned. "In any case, they seem to have what they wanted. The plane, the pilot, the inventor. All three.''

"But why?" asked Moira, her green eyes flashing. "And what about Edgar Tracey—how does he fit into all this?''

Frank glanced at Con Reilly, who shrugged his shoulders. "Naval Intelligence never heard of him," he said.

Frank nodded. "My guess is he's another Assassin agent.''

"I don't believe this!" Moira said, standing up and staring the others down, her face flushed with anger. "Your guesswork is full of holes! We still don't know what the Assassins could be up to or how Ray, my dad, and the MAX-1 fit into their plans!"

"You're right," said Con Reilly, brushing doughnut sugar off his hands and reaching for his coat. "Maybe it's just as well that you don't know."

He put on his coat and hat and looked sternly around the room at the young people. "From here on this is my case," he said in his gruffest, no-nonsense voice. He checked his watch. "I'm going back to work. From now on, I don't want to hear of any of you, and I mean *any*"—he looked hardest at Joe and Frank Hardy—"snooping around, putting yourselves in danger. If I do hear of any activity, young men, I'll have to book you. Is that understood?"

Frank nodded slowly. "Whatever you say, Con," he said as innocently as he could.

Reilly's mouth opened. He seemed somewhat surprised. Nevertheless, he straightened his hat, assured Moira that he'd let her know as soon as he heard anything, took a last doughnut, and left.

"Now what?" Jill asked, breaking the silence after Reilly left.

Frank considered. "I don't think we can take Con's advice," he said smoothly.

"Yeah," Joe interrupted. "Whatever's going on here is happening fast. By the time the authorities figure it out——"

"If they ever do," Frank added. "It could be too late. We've got to do something. The way I figure it, we have no choice."

"I know what that something is," said Moira. The others turned to look at her. Her green eyes were flashing, and her determined expression made her look strikingly like her father.

She hesitated, doing some rapid calculations. "I can have the MAX-2 ready to fly in three hours." She turned to Joe and Frank. "You two coming with me?" she asked.

"You bet!" Joe declared.

"We wouldn't miss it for the world!" Frank agreed.

Chapter

11

"THIS ONE'S BIGGER," Frank said after Moira had pulled the tarpaulin off the MAX-2.

The plane was hidden in a small hangar behind Lachlan's old-fashioned farmhouse. Max had kept this plane hidden for his own use, Moira had explained as she directed the Hardys out of Bayport and along a long, narrow country road. Last she'd heard, he hadn't perfected it.

"A bit bigger," Moira agreed. "This is supposed to be the family model. See the little backseat? Big enough for two kids—or one Hardy."

Flanked by Joe and Jill, Frank admired the sleek aircraft. It was a glossy metallic blue, rather than bright red like the MAX-1. "Was this one from an earlier design?" he asked, running a hand along the smooth finish.

"I think so," said Moira. "But he put it aside to design the MAX-1 for the backers. Then he went back to this later. See, you can tell this one isn't designed as well for speed and maneuverability."

"I'm surprised he didn't use the MAX-1's design," Joe said.

"He made up for it," Moira said. "See the extra engine under the tail fin? Dad put in one more thruster so the MAX-2 would be just as fast as its little brother. There are also an extra forty gallons in the fuel tank. The MAX-2 has a cruising range of fifteen hundred miles at a steady four hundred miles per hour."

"And that's on a regular, from-the-pump gasoline?" Jill asked incredulously.

"Well . . ." Moira smiled. "The MAX prefers premium when it can get it. But, yes, it will run on any normal automotive-grade fuel."

Frank ran his hands lovingly over the MAX-2's fiberglass and Kevlar fuselage. Its shape was slightly different from the MAX-1, but in its way, it was perfect, every line graceful and sleek. Moira noticed his appreciation.

"Dad overengineers everything. With powerful enough engines, the MAX-2 could easily hit Mach 2. That's twice the speed of sound," she explained for Jill.

Getting down to business, Moira assigned everyone a job to get the aircraft ready. As they were gassing up the airplane, she ran to her house to pick up a few things.

While she was gone, Jill moved closer to Joe. "I think you're making a big mistake," she told him.

"You mean by doing this thing ourselves?" he asked.

"No. By not taking me along!" she said, fuming.

Joe eyed her sympathetically. He was inclined to agree, for his own selfish reasons if nothing else. He really liked Jill, and it would be nice to have another pretty girl around. "I don't blame you," he said. "But it's too dangerous. Besides, as you can see, there's not enough room."

"I could sit on someone's lap," Jill insisted.

"Yeah, right." Joe laughed at the reporter's determination. "I'll tell you what. You stay home by the phone, and I promise we'll call you the minute we find out anything. You'll get a scoop big enough to get you hired by the *New York Times*. Who knows? You might even get a Pulitzer."

Jill grumbled a bit, but at least she was smiling, Joe noted as Moira returned wearing a form-fitting flight suit. Her arms were full of equipment. Joe whistled when he saw her, and Jill poked him with her elbow.

Moira tossed each of the Hardys a flight suit like hers. "These are Ray's," she said. "They should fit. I grabbed some cash from the safe, and I decided to bring this." She held up a sawed-off shotgun.

Frank frowned at the gun. "We don't work with guns, Moira."

Her eyes widened in surprise. "*They've* got them," she pointed out. "This isn't much of a gun, but it'll have to do." Pointedly, she marched over to the MAX-2 and stowed the shotgun under some equipment in the backseat. Jill and Joe exchanged glances. Moira looked so determined, no one dared object.

"Well, this doesn't mean we have to use it," Joe muttered to Jill.

Meanwhile, Moira had spread out a road atlas on the nose of the aircraft. Together, she and Frank traced their route cross-country. The International Expeditors' brochure claimed Nestor, Utah, as its home.

"Here it is," Frank said, pointing to a tiny black dot well away from the interstate highway.

Moira circled it with a red pen. "We should arrive in about eight hours," she said.

"Let's hope the solution to this mystery is there," Joe said.

They finished loading the MAX-2. Moira brought a cooler packed with sandwiches and sodas from the farmhouse. Finally she dragged over a bulky canvas sack and stuffed it behind the rear seat.

"What's that?" Joe asked.

"Another of my dad's inventions. A jetpack."

"You're kidding!"

"Nope. You strap it on your back and fly through the air. Just like Buck Rogers. It's much better than the one someone else designed a few years ago. You can stay aloft for ten minutes with ours. I'll show you how to use it on the way."

"If it's so good, why don't you take one along for each of you?" asked Jill.

"Because this is the only one in the world."

Joe stared at the pack, aware of how valuable the device must be. For that matter, so was the MAX-2. He realized that they were risking Max Lachlan's lifework on this adventure.

At last they were ready. Joe and Frank wheeled the MAX-2 out into the cold winter sunlight, Moira in the cockpit. She went through the computer checklist, making sure everything was in perfect working order. Then she gave the others a thumbs-up gesture.

"Let's do it," Frank said, climbing into the craft.

Jill hung back, her arms crossed over her chest, sulking. She was obviously still upset about being left out of the expedition.

Joe glanced at her before he climbed into the

MAX-2, and his heart melted. "Here," he said, tossing her the keys to the van. "Drive this back to our house and wait by the phone. I promise, we'll call you there."

Jill's face brightened a little. "Should I tell Con Reilly where you've gone?" she asked.

"Good idea. Wait a few hours, though, so we can get a head start. Then maybe he can arrange to get us some backup." He gave Jill a significant look. "Anyway, the authorities should know about this, just in case . . ."

Jill understood what Joe was getting at. Impulsively she walked up to Joe and gave him a quick hug. "You'd better come back, Joe Hardy," she murmured in his ear.

Blushing, Joe climbed into his place in the MAX-2 behind Frank and Moira. The aircraft's engines thrummed, and it rose straight up to a hundred feet before taking off like a shot.

As far as Frank was concerned, their time in the MAX-2 sped by as quickly as the miles. The MAX-2 was a joy to fly, if *flying* was the right word for it. Half the time, Moira skimmed along above the interstate. They were so low the aircraft might almost have been mistaken for a very lightweight car, except for its extraordinary speed and the fact that it passed *over* cars.

At other times they rocketed up into the sky,

chasing the sun westward. Although she was watching their fuel carefully, Moira allowed herself a few five-hundred-mile-per-hour dashes. Even at the limits of its speed capabilities, the cabin of the MAX-2 was amazingly quiet and comfortable.

"Want to drive?" Moira said casually to Frank an hour after takeoff.

Frank stared at her. "Sure."

"Go ahead." Smiling, Moira leaned back and let Frank take over the controls, instructing him in a calm, cool voice until he had it completely mastered. After that the two of them alternated piloting the craft. Frank had never enjoyed flying as much as he did that afternoon.

"Why are we flying so low?" Joe asked several hours later as Frank guided the plane over the interstate at three hundred miles per hour, keeping the plane just over the level of the telephone wires. Joe looked out the window and gulped at the sight of so much land speeding so fast just beneath them.

"To avoid other aircraft, and radar detection," Moira explained. "We don't want air traffic controllers calling us on the radio and, maybe, warning the guys in Utah that we're coming."

It was dusk as they began to follow an old, two-lane highway that ran beside Interstate 80 in Nebraska. Frank couldn't believe that even though they had flown more than twelve hundred miles, the engines still hummed softly. They glided down to a gas station at thirty miles per hour. Snow was piled up along the edges of the highway, but the road had been plowed clear.

Frank drifted the MAX-2 down to the gas pumps, settling it to a stop on its small, three-wheeled landing gear. A sandy-haired young man about Frank's age came out of the station to greet them. He wore overalls, a down vest, and a baseball cap.

"Howdy." The young man eyed the MAX-2 suspiciously.

"Fill 'er up, please," Frank said brightly as he, Moira, and Joe got out to stretch their legs.

"Better leave the pump running," Moira advised the young man. "It'll take a little more than a hundred gallons."

Joe watched the attendant gape at the MAX-2. He scratched the back of his neck and looked at them out of the corner of his eye. "You all from around here?" he asked.

"Nope," said Joe with a grin.

The young man was trying not to seem too curious, but he was bursting. "Uh, what kind of car did you say this is?"

"Didn't say," Joe answered.

"Well?"

"Oh, it's sort of an experimental model."

Joe pointed at Moira. "Her dad threw it together in his garage."

The young man's eyes nearly popped. "Is it fast?"

"Yeah, I guess so," Joe said casually. "Depends on what you compare it to."

The young man was getting very excited, though he tried not to show it. He looked around. The road was clear in both directions as far as he could see.

"Listen," he said to Joe. "I've got this car." He pointed to a black car with a flame paint job, parked next to the station. "It's a 'fifty-six Chevy, just about the fastest thing around here, blown big-block V-8, more than four hundred horsepower—"

"I see it," said Joe. "Looks nice. So?"

The young man's face split into a big, goofy grin. "So how'd you like to race?"

Chapter

12

"I CAN'T BELIEVE he agreed to this," Frank said to Moira.

"Lighten up, Frank," Joe said. "We've made good time. And this trip needs a little comic relief, right, Moira?"

Moira frowned impatiently. "I knew we'd have trouble if we kept you cooped up too long, Joe Hardy." She hesitated, then forced a smile. "Okay, sure. Let 'er rip!"

Joe leaned forward in the copilot's seat, while Moira tried to relax in the backseat. Frank was going to fly the plane, but Joe insisted on sitting next to him since he was the one who'd agreed to the race.

The kid with the car had told his buddy inside the station to cover for him, and now the two vehicles sat side by side on the empty road, pointing west. Their headlights lit the pavement, which stretched for over a mile without a curve.

"I can't believe this," Frank repeated under his breath as the kid gunned the engine of his Chevy. It burbled and rumbled, a big, crude, powerful monster of a car engine. "Drag racing on the way to meet up with the Assassins."

He turned to his brother, who was grinning from ear to ear. "You got us into this, partner. How do you want me to play it?"

"For laughs," Joe said, and looked straight up.

Frank wasn't sure what he meant. Then he caught on and started to laugh. Moira looked from one to the other, starting to get annoyed. "Come on," she said. "Let's get this over with."

Frank stared at the kid, who revved his engine, then glared straight ahead down the road, and floored it!

In that instant, Frank nailed it, too. But his engines were pointed down at the ground, and instead of racing the hot Chevy down the road, the MAX-2 shot straight up into the sky at three hundred feet per second. Frank hit the forward thrusters, and the MAX-2 shot past the Chevy. Whooping with glee, Joe looked down at the tiny racing headlights below.

"That was great!" Joe yelled, punching a fist into the air.

"You ain't seen nothing yet," his brother replied, straight-faced.

With that, he pointed the MAX-2's nose down, banked as he approached the road ahead of the speeding Chevy, then turned completely around so that the aircraft faced east. The MAX-2 shot forward again, and in a few seconds passed the racing Chevy again, *going in the opposite direction* five feet off the ground.

"Ha!" Moira cried, getting into the spirit of it in spite of herself. Frank then zoomed the aircraft skyward again and rocketed off into the night. "Did you see that kid's face? He's going to spend *years* trying to figure out what happened!"

As the MAX-2 headed west, the cockpit was filled with howls of laughter. "I'd give a million dollars for a picture of that kid's face," Frank said, grinning. "I've got to hand it to you, Joe. You do know how to lighten up a tense situation."

"No problem, Frank," Joe said. "Consider me your entertainment director."

In a few minutes they were all quiet and staring out the window. Joe thought of Jill, wishing she could be there.

Frank was thinking the same about Callie, and Moira about Ray.

* * *

Less than an hour later the MAX-2 crossed the border into Colorado. It cruised several hundred feet above the ground at four hundred miles per hour. Frank had the controls, but there wasn't much for him to do. Moira had showed him how to use a photoelectric sensor to lock the autopilot onto the reflective centerline of Interstate 76, so it took no effort to keep the plane on track.

Frank looked out at the flat, brown land below. The interstate ran parallel to the Platte River for nearly a hundred miles. Ahead, in the distance, loomed the Rocky Mountains. Crossing them without attracting the attention of the many military installations in the area would be the most difficult part of this flight, he realized.

He glanced over at Joe, who was snoozing in his bucket seat. Moira leaned forward, her pretty face popping out between the two headrests.

"Your brother sleeps a lot, huh?" she asked.

"Every chance he gets," Frank replied. They chuckled together. Then Moira turned serious.

"Frank," she said, "I don't know how to thank you for all your help."

"No need to, Moira. Ray's a friend, and that makes you one, too. He'd do the same for me."

"Are you sure?" She gazed out the windshield. "What if he really turns out to be one of these Assassins? I love him, Frank. But if he's done anything to hurt my father—"

"Look, Moira, we're just going to have to play things by ear. I don't think Ray's one of the bad guys. There's probably an explanation for everything that's happened, and we're going to find it. But until then, we've got to try not to worry too much. It'll work out. I know it."

His words seemed to make her feel better, and soon she was dozing in the backseat. Frank glanced over his shoulder at her. He was glad he'd been able to set her mind at ease, but he wished he felt as confident as he sounded.

When Joe woke up a bit later, he asked blearily, "Where are we?"

"Colorado—those are the Rockies dead ahead."

"What time is it?"

Frank indicated the clock on the dash. "Ten our time. Eight o'clock out here."

Joe rubbed his eyes with one hand and sat up, trying to wake up completely. After a while he turned to his brother. "How do you figure this one?" he asked.

Frank didn't need to ask what he was talking about. "It depends on what the Assassins would want the MAX-1 for. Once we know that—"

Joe interrupted him. "Hey, what's this?" He leaned closer to the dash. "Look. All the controls on this thing are clearly labeled, except this one." He pointed to a tiny switch half hidden under the dash. "Wonder what it does," Joe said.

Frank glanced over at it. Joe was right. It was unmarked. "Better not fiddle with it. We'll ask Moira when she wakes up—"

But before he could finish, Joe had reached over impetuously and flipped the little switch.

A buzzer sounded, startling Moira into wakefulness. "What? What is it?" she demanded.

"You tell me! You're the expert on this thing," Frank said. "Look—what's that all about?" He pointed to the windshield. Superimposed on it was an amber grid. In the grid flashed the phrase "Combat Mode?" Below that were two little boxes. One said yes, the other no.

Moira stared at the grid in surprise. "I have no idea what this is," she said softly. "It's not anything my dad ever mentioned."

"Let's test it out," said Joe, and touched the yes box.

Another buzzer sounded, and the grid changed. Now there were crosshairs superimposed on the grid. Underneath the crosshairs was the word *target*.

"Look at this!" Frank said. A joystick had popped out on the right side of his control grips. He moved the joystick around, and the crosshairs on the grid moved. "This is a gunsight! Is this thing armed?"

"No, of course not!" Moira snapped. "At least, I don't think so."

Meanwhile, another query had lit up on the amber grid. "Turboboost?" it asked. "Yes/No."

Joe turned to look at Moira. "Well?"

She shrugged. "I guess we give it a try. What do you think, Frank?"

In answer, Frank reached out and touched the yes box.

Suddenly the MAX-2 leapt forward, accelerating incredibly. The three of them were thrown back, pinned to their seats, as the airspeed indicator went wild. In a matter of seconds it showed that they had hit Mach 1.

The force of the acceleration overrode the autopilot. As they careened through the sky, Frank struggled with the controls. But the MAX-2 had a will of its own.

And there, looming dead ahead, miles in front of them but coming up fast at almost nine hundred miles an hour, were the Rockies!

Chapter

13

"I CAN'T SLOW IT DOWN!" Frank shouted to Moira. He struggled with the throttle and stick, but at these speeds the MAX behaved very differently. He couldn't get it to alter its course for the mountainside.

"Keep trying!" Moira ordered. She scrunched up between the two bucket seats, reaching for the dash. She hit a panel, which dropped open, exposing the onboard computer system. "I'll try to find a system override for the last command!"

They were almost into the mountainside. "Watch out!" Joe yelled, clenching his fists.

Desperate, Frank yanked back hard on the stick. To his surprise, the nose rose at an eighty-degree angle, a nearly vertical climb. "I think I've got it," he said excitedly as he, Joe, and Moira were flattened back against their seats by the gravity force. He pulled harder on the control stick, staring at the mountain peak just ahead.

"Will we miss it?" Moira yelled.

Frank didn't answer. His knuckles were white. The aircraft reached the mountain—and then they were over it, skimming so near its peak that Joe could make out individual small boulders in the snow on the top.

"Whew," he muttered, unclenching his fists. "A thrill a minute, riding this machine."

The plane was still climbing at supersonic speed, and the g-forces were enormous. Moira grimaced as she struggled to keep working on the computer. She hit one more programming sequence. Suddenly the turboboost cut off, and the MAX-2 dropped back down to subsonic speed.

His heart pounding, Frank leveled the MAX-2 out, throttled back, and finally stopped the plane in a midair hover. Then Frank took it down in a vertical descent to the mountain below. It settled comfortably into the snow.

"Everybody okay?" he asked. They both nodded. Then he quietly asked, "What was that all about?"

Moira shook her head, bewildered. "Honestly, I don't know. My dad never said anything about putting such powerful engines into this plane.''

Joe broke in. ''Isn't there something you're both forgetting about?'' He pointed to the grid on the windshield, where the crosshairs still blinked. ''How about trying this, too? I'm getting tired of surprises.''

Frank and Moira looked at each other. ''Okay, if you say so,'' Frank said grimly. He expertly lifted the MAX-2 back into the sky.

''What's our target?''

Joe pointed back toward the mountain. ''That nice big boulder down there. See if you can take it out.''

''We don't even know what we're armed with,'' Moira said nervously. ''Guns? Missiles?''

''Only one way to find out.'' Frank flew the plane several miles past the mountain, then turned back toward it. He moved the joystick until the crosshairs lined up on the boulder Joe had picked out. ''Now what?'' he said.

The screen told him immediately. ''Correct target?'' it asked. ''Yes/No.''

Frank nodded to his brother, and Joe touched the yes box. The message changed. ''Target locked. Predicted accuracy 99%,'' it said. Then it changed once more. ''Commence firing? Yes/No.''

Joe turned to his big brother, then to Moira.

Both looked determined. Joe pressed the yes box.

As Moira and the Hardys watched, a thin beam of intense white light flashed out from the nose of the MAX-2 and struck the boulder, which exploded in a burst of light!

"An energy-beam weapon!" Joe said as the craft streaked past the mountaintop. He was almost beside himself. "Your dad really *is* Buck Rogers, Moira! He built himself a death ray! These things aren't supposed to exist for another twenty years or so!"

"It sounds fantastically expensive to develop," Moira said doubtfully. "I don't see how he could afford to produce that kind of weapon."

"Maybe somebody gave it to him," Joe suggested. "Maybe the government is backing him on this—or maybe it was stolen from the government," he added hesitantly.

"One thing's for sure," Frank said after he'd set the plane back on course. "This plane is a lot different from its advance billing. This is no family sedan. It's a supersonic fighter of incredible speed, armed with an amazingly destructive energy-beam weapon. The MAX series may be the deadliest aircraft in the world."

"And one of them may be in the hands of the Assassins!" Joe added.

It was just past ten at night as Joe stared down at the vast, empty desert of Utah, sparkling in the light of a three-quarter moon. The MAX-2 skimmed the desert at just a few hundred feet. Joe shifted in his seat, wondering if they'd ever get there.

"What are those things?" Moira asked, pointing at some masses of rock that looked like gigantic tree stumps rising up from the desert floor.

"Buttes," Frank explained. "They can get up to several hundred feet high. Once they were hills, but hundreds of thousands of years of desert winds have carved them into those shapes. Want to take a closer look?"

He brought the MAX-2 down, settling it on top of one of the largest formations. As soon as Frank cut the engines, Joe popped the canopy and leapt out onto solid ground.

"Boy, oh, boy, nothing like a lungful of cool desert air," he said, breathing deeply.

"Actually, I landed here for a reason." Frank followed his brother out onto the surface of the butte, and Moira followed, stretching her arms and legs. "It's getting late. We're just about a hundred and fifty miles from Nestor, but I don't know if we could find it in the dark. How about waiting till dawn so we can see what the setup is before we land?"

"What do we do till then?" Moira demanded.

"Eat. Sleep."

"The Hardys' two favorite pastimes." A

flicker of impatience crossed Moira's delicate face, but she quickly relented. "Okay. You're right. Let's break out the sandwiches."

Moira had packed sleeping bags in case they were gone for a while. After they'd eaten, Frank and Joe took their bags and climbed out onto the butte. Moira would sleep in the MAX-2, but for now she climbed out with them to take a look around.

Joe sat hunched under his jacket, looking out at the spectacular view. The desert was chilly, but not anywhere as cold as Bayport had been. The sky was absolutely cloudless, and the moon and stars lit the scene as well as city lights could have. The desert seemed endless, hundreds of buttes receding toward the horizon.

"It's so beautiful here," Moira said with a sigh. "I wish Ray were with us." For a moment Joe thought she was going to cry, but she pulled herself together. Some time later she stood up and wished them both a good night. She climbed back into the MAX-2 and settled down to sleep.

"She's terrific," Joe said to Frank. "I hope when this is all over she doesn't end up hurt."

"However things fall tomorrow, we keep an eye on her, right?" Frank said.

Joe nodded in silence. Then he added quietly, "Anything could happen tomorrow if the Assassins are involved. You think we're making a mistake doing this on our own?"

Frank thought about it. "It's kind of late to get in touch with the Network." The Network was the "good guys." The Hardys had worked on a number of cases with them. "Besides," Frank continued, "everything's been happening really fast. Whatever the Assassins are planning could happen any minute. I don't see how we can afford to wait for help. Anyway," he added, indicating the MAX-2, "we have *that*. If we can knock out the MAX-1 while it's still on the ground, we should be able to handle anything else they throw at us."

He stretched his arms and yawned. "Let's hit the sack," he said. "We have a big day tomorrow."

They hunkered down into their sleeping bags, and the next thing Joe knew, it was morning.

Dawn was just beginning to break behind them as Frank angled the MAX-2 low over the desert. As they'd covered the last hundred miles of their journey, Frank had experimented with the combat capabilities of the aircraft. He and Moira had taken turns operating it at supersonic speeds.

Joe had tested its computers with the combat command in place. He found that the amber grid projected on the windshield could magnify a target, provide a radar image, or break down a scene into simple graphics, like a video game.

For fun, he'd put a radar- and computer-generated image of Nestor up in a corner of the windshield, even as the real place grew before their eyes.

Frank flew flat out without turboboost, doing five hundred miles per hour barely ten feet off the desert floor. Ahead lay a truck stop. He could see the old neon Diner sign. There was a parking lot, the old-fashioned silver diner itself, an old clapboard house, three run-down mobile homes, a few gas pumps, and a big corrugated metal garage.

"They've probably got the STOL and the MAX-1 hidden in there," Frank said. "We'll hit the garage first, then see if they're ready to talk."

He banked the MAX-2, shot up into the sky, wheeled the plane around, and came swooping in fast. The combat-mode lights blinked amber on the windshield. Frank lined up the garage in the crosshairs.

Suddenly the MAX-2 began to slow down.

"What's happening?" Frank played the controls, but the plane refused to respond to his commands. On the windshield the amber projections of the combat mode winked out. Moira, in the seat beside him, flipped the hidden switch several times, without result.

"This is just what happened when I was flying the MAX-1 with Ray!" Frank exclaimed.

"It's remote control," said Moira. "They must have a radio control unit that's overriding our own systems!"

From the backseat Joe demanded, "What do we do now?"

"You stay down!" his brother commanded. "Throw a sleeping bag over your head."

Despite Frank's and Moira's struggles, the MAX-2 slowed to a stop directly over the desert truck stop. It hovered there for a moment. Then, engines whining, it began to descend. Frank hit the switches frantically, trying to get the plane to respond to him, but the MAX-2 continued its descent. Finally it settled gently down onto the parking lot next to the diner. A dark blue jeep was parked in the lot.

Frank and Moira looked out. The two men in crew cuts were waiting for them with AK-47 assault rifles pointed at the MAX-2.

"All right, you two, get out slowly," one of the men ordered.

Frank and Moira climbed out of the MAX-2, hands held high above their heads. One of the men approached them.

"Nice to see you again, Hardy," he said, hitting Frank in the stomach with the butt of his rifle. Frank fell to his knees, gasping.

"Frank!" Moira cried. Then she turned to the man. "Leave him alone!" she yelled at him. "Haven't you done enough? What have done with Ray? Where's my father?"

"Here I am, sweetheart," said Max Lachlan.

Frank looked up as Moira, startled, exclaimed, "Dad!"

"Such concern from a daughter makes a father's heart glad."

Max Lachlan stepped out of the diner. He looked relaxed and healthy. Frank's gaze fell to the Browning high-powered automatic in his right hand. In his left hand rested a remote control unit no larger than a cigarette pack. He held it up for Frank and Moira to admire.

"Doesn't this work splendidly? I must thank you two for delivering the second MAX."

Chapter

14

"I CAN'T BELIEVE IT!" Moira stared at her father. "You're one of them!"

"The last time we saw you, Lachlan, you'd just had a heart attack. You've recovered quickly," Frank said coldly.

"Yes, well, all it takes is a little amyl nitrate to simulate one of those." Lachlan smiled. "Within a few hours it all wears off and you feel fine."

"Why, Dad?" Moira's voice trembled. "Why'd you fake a heart attack?"

The white-haired man turned to his daughter. "It was your fault," he said irritably. "I was going to leave with my friends here"—he indicated the two gunmen—"when you barged in. I had to do something to distract you so they could escape. I thought it was quite clever on their part to kidnap me from the hospital.''

He scowled at the girl and at Frank. "You should have stayed out of this, Moira. You, too, Hardy. I tried to get you to leave it alone, but you wouldn't take no for an answer. By the way, Hardy, where's your brother?''

Frank thought fast. "Back in Bayport,'' he answered. "If he doesn't hear from us in two hours, he's supposed to tell the police that we came out here. There'll be state troopers swarming all over this place.''

Lachlan laughed a low, rumbling laugh. "You really expect me to believe that? I know the reputation you two have. No way he'd let you go on an adventure like this by yourself.'' He addressed the two gunmen. "Herb, Bernie, check the MAX-2.''

Buried beneath the pile of sleeping bags in the back of the MAX-2, Joe listened, holding his breath. Frank had left the canopy partway open, so that Lachlan's voice came through clearly. The gunmen were on their way! It would take them less than a minute to find him.

Quickly, Joe burrowed deeper under the pile of equipment, trying to make his six-foot frame invisible as the sound of footsteps approached the aircraft. He knew that he was Frank and Moira's only chance of escape, but to help them he had to elude his searchers and then get out of the plane.

Just then Joe heard a scuffling noise coming from near the diner. It sounded like a chopping noise. Then he heard Frank grunt, followed by the sound of someone falling to the ground. "Watch out!" came Lachlan's voice from the other side of the lot. Joe raised his head and peered over the edge of the cockpit. Frank had attacked one of the gunmen!

"Moira, get down!" Frank shouted as Max Lachlan fired two rounds from his big automatic. The shots came so close that Frank wondered whether Lachlan meant to miss him.

"Freeze!" Lachlan shouted. Frank froze, and so did Moira. The fallen gunman picked himself up, glaring at Frank. He whacked Frank across the side of the head with the barrel of his rifle. "That's enough, Bernie!" Lachlan commanded.

The blow staggered Frank, but he stayed on his feet. Lachlan spoke again. "Mr. Hardy here will be useful to us intact. But if he makes another move, you have my permission to shoot him. Now see if his brother's in that aircraft!"

Bernie kept his rifle trained on Frank as Herb climbed into the MAX-2. He poked among the sleeping bags in the back with the muzzle of his assault rifle. He came up empty. "No one here," he called to Lachlan.

* * *

The moment Joe saw Frank grab Bernie's rifle, he moved. He knew Frank was giving him his only chance, and he'd better make the most of it.

Joe rolled over and out of the MAX-2, falling to the side away from the fight. Flat on the ground, he kept rolling. There was some scrub brush on the edge of the parking lot. It wasn't good cover, but it would have to do.

When he was reasonably well hidden, Joe risked another look. Herb had checked the MAX-2 and found it empty. Then Lachlan spoke to Frank and Moira, but now Joe was too far away to hear what was said. He scanned the little cluster of buildings, trying to decide which one was most likely to have a telephone. Probably the diner, he decided. Now, how could he get to it without being spotted?

"I still don't think your brother's in Bayport," Lachlan said to Frank, carefully avoiding his daughter's eye. "But we'll deal with him if and when he shows up. Meanwhile, our plans will have run their course in a few hours. By then it'll be far too late for anyone to stop us."

"What plans?" Frank asked.

Lachlan looked startled. Then he laughed. "You'd love to know, wouldn't you?" He glanced at his watch, then back at Frank. "Well, you're not going anywhere, and we have time to talk. Why not tell you?"

Frank looked over at Moira, who stared, unblinking, straight ahead.

"The MAX needs a suitable test to prove its worth to the people who financed its development. That test will take place a few hundred miles from here, near Edwards Air Force Base."

"The space shuttle . . ." Frank said. "It's returning to Cape Canaveral—and the president is going to be on board!"

Lachlan beamed at him. "Bright boy. You'd have had a wonderful future if you'd left me alone. That big, slow 747 is a sitting duck with the shuttle strapped to its back."

"You want to kill the president?" Moira asked, horrified. "But, Dad, why? Why are you doing any of this?"

"Vengeance," Frank said softly. Finally everything he'd been told about Max Lachlan was coming together.

"And don't forget power," Lachlan added calmly. "Never forget power. That fool was responsible for my wife's death, and I was powerless to prevent it."

"Dad, that's crazy. The president didn't kill Mom!"

Again Frank had the answer. "He wasn't the president then. He was the head of NASA. He personally rejected your Shuttle design, didn't he, Max?"

"He didn't give me enough time!" Lachlan

snapped. "He bankrupted me. Without money, I couldn't afford to test my prototype aircraft adequately. When Ellen insisted on taking the first flight with me, we crashed and she died! Whose fault is it if not his? Now, today, after all these years, he'll pay!"

"Max, you've been suckered," Frank said. "You were the perfect patsy for the Assassins."

"I'm no patsy," Lachlan sneered. "This is a business arrangement. They have money and power, and I have designs. We were meant for each other!"

"Dad, you'll never get away with it," Moira said, her eyes darkly anxious. "Please, Dad, stop now, before you've hurt anyone." She gasped as a new thought struck her. "What have you done with Ray?" she demanded.

Her father's expression relaxed. "Interesting that you should put those two thoughts together, Moira," he said. "Of course I'll get away with it. You see, as far as the world is concerned, Ray will be the assassin. I'll just be another unfortunate victim—like Frank Hardy and my own daughter."

Lachlan fastened his narrowed eyes on his daughter, and Frank read only madness there. Lachlan no longer really knew who she was. "You two are going to be blasted from the sky by Ray when you try to stop him from killing the president," he explained.

* * *

Joe began working his way around the edge of the truck-stop area to avoid being spotted. At last he was behind one of the windworn mobile homes. He stood, peering cautiously in through a window. The trailer was empty except for a half-dozen cots. There didn't seem to be a telephone. Joe moved on.

When he reached the corrugated garage, he put his ear to the wall. He could hear voices inside. The rest of International Expeditors' friendly engineering staff, he guessed. He found a window and peeked in. Three men in coveralls were bustling about the red MAX-1. The big STOL was also in the garage, concealed from prying eyes. One of the engineers glanced toward the window. Joe ducked.

No one was looking for him. When he felt it was safe to move again, Joe made a hunched-over dash to the back of the diner. Once again he took a cautious look through a window.

Pay dirt! There was a phone on the countertop. Unfortunately, there was also another engineer armed with an assault rifle, eating a hamburger three feet away.

The engineer sat bathed in a beam of sunlight falling straight down on him. There was a skylight directly over the man, and it was open! If Joe could get up on the roof of the diner . . .

As the engineer wolfed down his hamburger, a shadow fell over him. A passing cloud? He looked up. Joe Hardy crouched in the skylight, grinning down at him. Before the engineer could move, Joe dropped, smashing the other man's head into the counter and knocking him unconscious.

Joe leapt to the floor and reached for the phone. But before he reached it he heard a muffled voice coming from behind the counter. He looked over it. A man was sitting on the floor, bound and gagged.

"Ray!" he said. "What are you doing there?"

He vaulted over the counter and yanked the gag out of Ray's mouth.

"Lachlan's an Assassin! He's going to kill the president!" Ray announced.

Joe's quick mind put things together as rapidly as his brother's had. "They're going to use the MAX to shoot down his plane?"

"Yes! Untie me. We've got to stop them!"

Joe untied Ray and, as Ray rubbed his ankles and wrists, reached again for the phone.

"Who are you calling?" Ray asked.

"Um, a secret agency," Joe hedged.

"The Network?" Ray startled Joe by taking the receiver from him and beginning to dial.

"Let me," said Ray. "They're expecting my call."

Max Lachlan gestured with his automatic. "That's enough talking," he said. "We've got a busy morning ahead of us. Let's put you two someplace where you'll stay out of trouble until then."

Moira began to cry. "Daddy, please," she pleaded. "It's not too late yet. Don't do it!"

For the first time a look of fleeting sorrow passed across Max Lachlan's face, and for a moment he looked almost sane. "I'm sorry, Moira. When your mother died, I died, too. Now there's nothing but hate left. And you're in my way." His voice hardened, and his eyes glazed over again. "Now move!"

He marched them to the diner, with Herb and Bernie following.

The door of the diner opened just then, and Ray and Joe stepped out. Ray held the assault rifle. Max Lachlan and his henchmen gaped at them, amazed. Ray leveled his weapon at Lachlan.

"It's all over, Max," he said. "Give it up."

Max Lachlan slowly lowered his automatic, his face a picture of defeat and dejection. Then, in a movement too sudden to follow, he dropped into a crouch, aimed his automatic at Ray, and squeezed off three lightning-quick rounds.

Chapter

15

"AAGHH!" Next to Joe, Ray grunted and reeled back. One of Lachlan's shots had grazed his shoulder. Herb and Bernie raised their assault rifles, but Ray recovered enough to aim a quick burst of fire, and Bernie fell to the ground.

In the same instant, Frank turned and scooped up Bernie's assault rifle. As Herb and Max Lachlan dashed for cover, Frank grabbed Moira by the arm and pulled her off in the opposite direction. They found cover beside the MAX-2.

"Come on!" Joe yelled to Ray, leading him back into the diner. Inside, Joe poked his head up to look out a window.

The noise of Herb's rifle made him duck

again, but not before he saw Frank step out from behind the MAX-2.

"Watch it!" Joe's warning came too late. A shot rang out from the direction of the garage, and a bullet whizzed by Frank's ear. He dropped, rolled, and looked up to see three "engineers" clustered between the open bay doors, each holding an AK-47.

Lachlan called out to them, "Cover us!" Two of the gunmen began firing in Frank's direction, while the third blasted away at the diner, forcing Joe to duck back down.

"Stand back, Joe!" Ray shouted. "The bullet only grazed me. I can cover it from here."

Lachlan and Herb sprinted for the nearest of the mobile homes. They reached the door, but one of Ray's bullets caught Herb in the thigh. The Assassin yelped and staggered. Lachlan pulled him through the door.

Frank turned to Moira, sweat trickling down his face. "Bernie's down. When I say go, you run for the diner," he ordered.

A few seconds later, after surveying the scene, Frank shouted, "Go!" Moira dashed for the diner. Ray, seeing Moira's dash for cover, sent a burst of gunfire toward the men crowded in the garage. Frank, sensing the time was right, followed Moira.

A shot from the mobile home kicked up dust at Frank's feet. Ray covered his friend, firing a burst at the trailer. Moira stumbled the last few feet to the door of the diner, and then she was in, followed immediately by Frank. Outside, Bernie lay in the dirt, groaning.

"Ray!" Moira cried, rushing to her fiancé's side. She threw her arms around him.

"Hey, Moira." He embraced her with his left arm. His wounded right arm hung uselessly at his side. "Joe tells me you're responsible for this heroic rescue." He grinned and kissed her.

"Some rescue," she said. "We're trapped here."

"Not exactly," said Frank. "All we've got to do is stalemate them until the president and the shuttle are out of range."

Moira bandaged Ray's wound as well as she could with rags, while Frank asked, "So how do *you* figure into all this, pal?"

"He's a Network agent," Joe said.

"You're a what?" Moira exclaimed.

"It's a long story, Mo," Ray said.

"I thought you got kicked out of the navy," said Frank.

"That was my cover," Ray told him. "The Network recruited me through Naval Intelligence. They needed a pilot to infiltrate Max's operation. I had to look dirty. So we got me a dishonorable discharge."

"What did Max do to catch the Network's attention?" Frank wanted to know.

"A few things," Ray replied. "His finances were screwy. There were rumors that the MAX series' guidance systems were awfully similar to a top-secret system that only the government was supposed to have. Then some directed-energy weapon designs were stolen by the Assassins. The Network traced them to Max."

"You mean the death ray?" Joe asked.

Ray nodded.

"What *is* that thing? How does it work?" Frank asked.

"It's a laser. *Star Wars* technology. It was originally supposed to be mounted on satellites to knock out incoming ICBMs."

"I knew it!" Frank said. But his glance caught something out the window, and his smile faded. "Uh-oh," he said, pointing.

The others followed his gaze. One of the engineers was creeping toward the diner on his belly, holding his rifle out in front of him.

"I'll take care of this," Ray said. He aimed carefully and shot one round. It hit the dirt a foot in front of the engineer's nose. The man looked up, goggle-eyed. "The next one takes your nose off!" Ray shouted. "Freeze and drop your weapon!"

Heavy fire erupted from the garage and the mobile home. Bullets tore through the walls of the diner. The Hardys, Moira, and Ray flattened out on the floor to keep from being hit.

Then, as suddenly as it began, the gunfire stopped.

Cautiously they looked out. The engineer on the ground lay still. He had been struck by a stray shot from his own men.

Frank turned back to Ray. "You had a scrapbook on the Assassins."

"Homework," Ray answered. "Know thine enemy. I wasn't even sure until Saturday whether Max was in tight with them or just doing a single job. I was waiting to see what he'd do." He chuckled wryly. "Obviously I didn't expect this."

"How'd he get you?" Joe asked.

"When Mo and I called him from the pizza joint that night, he asked me to meet him back at the hangar after I dropped Mo off at home. I walked right into a trap."

"How does he expect to get away with this?" Moira said. "I can't believe he's my father."

"He's not, right now," Frank cut in. "He's unbalanced. He set Ray up from the start. Ray's dishonorable discharge could appear to be a motive. Your father could take Ray up in the MAX-1, use it to shoot down the president, then land in the desert. He'd get out, then use the remote control to crash the MAX-1 into the mountainside, with Ray in it. They'd find him wandering around a few hours later, saying Ray stole his aircraft and kidnapped him to fix it after Saturday's malfunction.''

"Nobody would believe that, would they?" Moira asked Ray.

Ray shrugged. "Maybe. If not, the story would at least hold up for a week or two. If it began to fall apart, Max could disappear into the Assassin underground. If it was accepted, he could go on as before, making millions from selling MAX aircraft. Either way, he'd come out on top.''

"But not anymore," Joe said. "We've got him beat. Here come those Network reinforcements!''

A pair of army jeeps painted in tan camouflage rolled into the little truck stop. One of them was armed with twin fifty-caliber machine guns, while the second mounted a recoilless cannon.

Then Joe spotted an enormous black Mercedes limousine with dark-tinted windows. It pulled in off the highway and stopped, its engine idling, as it sat behind the jeeps in the truck-stop parking lot. For a moment no one moved.

Ray pulled himself up to the window and peered out. "Funny," he said. "I was expecting them to *fly* in—" Then he stopped, obviously remembering something. "Wait a second! Max told me he was expecting some important guests who wanted to 'watch the show.' ''

Outside, a hatch popped open in the lead half-track, and two men climbed out. They were armed with AK-47s. Each of them wore sunglasses and scanned the truck stop suspiciously.

At the other window Frank groaned. "We've got a big problem, folks. Those aren't Network agents. *They're Assassins!*"

Chapter

16

"THEY PLANNED to abandon this place once Max and I took off in the MAX-1," Ray said. "They'd load everything, even the jeeps, into the STOL. Max joked that it would make a wonderful viewing platform for the assassination."

"Who's in the limo?" Joe wondered.

"Doesn't matter," Frank answered. "We can't stay here. Any second now Lachlan's going to shout a warning to them. Is there a back way out of here?" he asked his brother.

Before they had time to act, Joe saw Max Lachlan at the door of the mobile home. He shouted a few words at the Assassins in front of the jeeps and pointed to the diner.

"Now we're in for it," Joe said.

Ray winged a shot in Lachlan's direction, and he ducked back under cover. But now the two Assassins leapt for cover behind the lead jeep and opened fire. They pointed and shouted, and the big guns began to turn ominously toward the diner.

"Folks, we've gotta move!" Frank shouted.

The group ran to the back window. Joe and Moira slipped outside, followed by Ray. But just as Frank hit the ground behind the diner, the big guns erupted.

Joe, Frank, Moira, and Ray flattened out on the ground as fifty-caliber slugs and explosive shells tore into the building.

At last the firing stopped. Still half deafened, Joe lifted his head to inspect the damage. The diner had been torn to shreds, but miraculously, none of them had been hit. Joe started to stand up. Then he saw one of the engineers standing over them—and the muzzle of his AK-47 was less than an inch from Joe's nose.

The engineer marched the four of them out to the parking lot. Max and Herb had emerged from the mobile home. Lachlan was furious. Before his henchmen could bring the Hardys to him, he sprang at them, swinging his big, hamlike fists at Frank.

"Hey!" Joe yelled, moving to help his brother. An engineer smashed the butt of his rifle into Joe's back, knocking him to his knees.

"Dad, stop, you'll kill him!" Moira cried.

"He's dead already. You all are!" Lachlan ranted. "How dare you try to stop me—"

Suddenly the lead jeep exploded!

"The Network!" Joe cried, looking up as three big helicopters—an Apache attack ship, a Huey gunship, and a Chinook transport—swooped in. A rocket from the Apache had caught the open car dead center.

All was pandemonium as the Gatling gun in the Huey spewed hundreds of rounds at the Assassins' vehicles. The Assassins scrambled for cover.

As Max Lachlan gaped in impotent rage, Frank threw a quick right uppercut to the big man's belly. Lachlan grunted with pain. Frank caught him with a strike to the temple.

"Ray, Moira, let's go," Joe yelled over the gunfire.

They scrambled for cover as the Chinook helicopter landed, disgorging a score of flak-jacketed Network agents armed with M-16 rifles and Mac-10 submachine pistols. The two other choppers circled overhead.

"Look!" Ray shouted to Joe, pointing toward the limousine. It was backing out of the parking lot. A Network agent stood with his back to it, firing his M-16. The limousine drove right over him.

"Where's Frank?" Joe yelled back, looking wildly around.

Frank was still locked in a fight with Max Lachlan. Max outweighed Frank by fifty pounds, much of it muscle, and he was an experienced street fighter. Frank hit Max twice for every blow Max landed, but Moira's father seemed indestructible.

As Joe started toward his brother, he noticed a Network agent launch a grenade after the speeding limousine. Joe paused to watch the grenade explode in front of the black car. The limousine careened out of control, its driver dead. Joe saw the direction it was headed and screamed, "Frank! Look out!"

Frank ducked beneath Max's blows and glanced up to see the huge car coming out of the smoke, headed straight for them. "Watch it!" he yelled at Lachlan.

Lachlan turned toward the car and cried out, but he was too late. As Frank leapt back, the car knocked Max over like a bowling pin, and rolled to a stop several yards away.

Unhurt, Frank sprinted to where he'd seen Max go down. "Where is he?" Joe asked, joining him. Max had disappeared!

By now the firing had died down. The battle was over. Dazed, Frank and Joe surveyed the destruction, still hoping to spot Max.

The Network agents were gathering the Assassins into a small, sullen cluster. The Assassins' vehicles were wrecked. The Huey gunship hovered over the scene like a wary dragon. The Chinook sat in the parking lot, its rotors spinning slowly. The Apache had disappeared over the nearby hills.

"Well, brother, we made it again," Joe said in the silence. "Moira and Ray are over there." He pointed toward the diner. "Now all we need is Max."

"The agents must have caught him," Frank said, still somewhat dazed. But before the brothers could continue their search, a familiar voice caught their attention.

"Hardys—over here." Joe and Frank turned. Emerging from the Chinook was Edgar Tracey. He was dressed in military fatigues. He wore mirrored sunglasses, and a .45 automatic was strapped to his side. "I thought I told you two to keep out of this," he said. Then he smiled and held out his hand. "Little joke. You've done very well."

Joe looked at him suspiciously. "Who are you really?" he demanded.

"I'm the guy who recruited your friend Ray for the Network," Tracey responded.

"Where's the Gray Man? He's our Network contact," Frank said.

"The Network didn't want to contact you." Tracey grinned. "We didn't want you involved in this one. And we knew if you saw the Gray Man in Bayport, you'd know something was up."

Joe spoke up. "Um, I think we may have blown your cover. The Bayport Police have some pictures of you."

Tracey pulled a roll of film from his shirt pocket. "You mean the roll Miss Stern, the reporter, took? Funny how this sort of thing can disappear from a locked evidence room. My secret is safe."

"If you didn't want us involved, why did Ray call me?" Frank demanded.

"Because he's an inexperienced agent, and you're his friend. He made a mistake. I tried to cover for him by scaring you off."

"We don't scare off," said Joe.

"So I've noticed."

Tracey surveyed the prisoners. "Quite a haul." He spotted a man in a black suit being led away from the limousine by two agents. "Incredible," Tracey said.

"Who's he?" Joe asked.

"I knew if we bided our time, Lachlan would lead us to some big fish. But I never expected the number-three man in the Assassin organization to turn up in my net! With him and Lachlan out of action—" He looked around. "By the way, where *is* Lachlan?"

"We thought your men had him."

Just then the MAX-1 roared out of the garage with Lachlan at the controls. The Huey gunship moved to block its way. A thin beam of light lanced out of the nose of the MAX-1, and the Huey crashed to the ground, a mass of twisted metal.

"He's going for it!" shouted Joe.

Moira came running across the lot toward them. "I can stop him," she yelled. "I have the remote control!" She held it up, turning its knobs and dials. "No! It's not working!" She turned to them. "I found it on the ground. He must have dropped it during all the shooting, but it's broken!"

"Don't worry," snapped Tracey. "We still have two Apaches out there. He won't get past them!"

"Don't be so sure of that, Tracey," Frank said. "You don't know what the MAX-1 can do! Come on, Joe. We've got to go after him!"

"Me, too!" Moira insisted.

"Not this time," Joe told her. "You've got a wounded boyfriend to take care of. Frank can handle it!"

The two Hardys dashed to the MAX-2 and clambered in.

As soon as they were aloft, Joe and Frank began scanning the sky for the MAX-1. "Where's Edwards Air Force Base?" Joe asked.

Frank pointed to the southwest. "About four hundred miles that way. Max can catch the president's plane midway between here and there. Look!" He pointed. Down below, hugging the ground, was MAX-1. As they watched, Lachlan hit the turboboost, and the MAX-1 rocketed away at supersonic speed.

"There are the two Apaches," Joe said, indicating two predatory shapes swooping toward them. "They must have spotted him, too."

"Too bad they didn't catch him," said Frank. "They're tough birds—armed to the teeth—but they can't match Max's speed. I guess it's up to us. Let's go."

Frank started to bank in pursuit of the MAX-1. He expected the two Apaches to veer off, but instead they kept coming, straight for the MAX-2.

"What's wrong with those chopper jocks? Can't they tell the difference between the MAX-1 and the MAX-2?" shouted Frank. Then realization dawned on his face. "Didn't Tracey tell them to go after the *red* one?"

As if in answer, the lead chopper launched a pair of missiles straight for them!

"They've mistaken us for Lachlan!" Joe yelled. "Let's get out of here!"

"Those are Sidewinder missiles he just fired," Frank yelled back. "No way we can outrun them. Now we're really in for it!"

Chapter

17

FRANK HIT THE TURBOBOOST. "Hold tight," he told his brother grimly. "Now the ride really gets wild!"

The MAX-2 sprang forward instantly, the g-forces pinning the Hardys back into their seats.

"Can we outrun them?" Joe asked.

"No way. Those things fly at four times the speed of sound! But I've bought us some time, and maybe I can use it."

He glanced over his shoulder, calculating. He could see the missiles on his tail. The Apache helicopters were already far behind. If he could elude this first attack, they wouldn't have another shot at him.

Frank used all the MAX-2's amazing maneuverability to dip, turn, and spin, trying to escape the two missiles.

"This is it, Joe. If this doesn't work, we've had it!" In one last, desperate attempt, Frank stopped the MAX-2 in midair, suddenly reversing its engine thrust. He followed that up instantly with a straight drop, one hundred feet in a fraction of a second.

Even the Sidewinder missiles couldn't match this tactic. They whizzed by, a hundred feet above the MAX-2.

To Frank, the amber grid on the windshield looked just like the screen of a video game, and now he brought all his arcade mastery into play. He aimed and fired, aimed and fired. The laser beam lanced out from the nose of the MAX-2 once, twice—both missiles exploded in midair.

"You did it!" Joe shouted, slapping his brother's shoulder.

Frank sighed with relief. But an instant later he was composed and businesslike again.

"That takes care of that," he said. "Now let's go get Lachlan!" He nailed the controls, and the MAX-2 rocketed off in pursuit of its prey.

"We should be able to spot the MAX-1 from here," Frank said as he brought the plane up to ten thousand feet.

As the brothers searched the sky below, they

heard a roar building behind them. At the same time a voice hailed them over the radio.

"This is Bravo Leader calling MAX-2. Do you read me? Over." Suddenly they were flanked by a pair of Air Force F-16 fighters. The big birds of prey looked sleek and awesome, dwarfing the Hardys' aircraft.

Frank responded. "I read you, Bravo Leader. Over."

"Good deal. Down below they say you've done fine, but now you can leave the wrap-up to the professionals. That's us, MAX-2. Over."

"We'd just as soon come along for the ride," Frank responded. "Over."

"Suit yourself, MAX-2. But it's gonna be all over by the time you get there. Over."

"Listen, Bravo Leader. The MAX-1 is tougher than you think. Be careful. Over."

"Sonny, you've got to be kidding. Over." The two jets hit their afterburners and blasted off past the MAX-2 as though it were standing still.

"Pretty impressive," said Joe.

"They'd better be," Frank said through gritted teeth.

Ten minutes and a hundred miles later, now in Nevada skies, Joe exclaimed, "You were right, Frank! Look!" Two parachutes hung in the air, drifting gently downward. On the floor of the desert lay the two F-16s, crashed and burning.

"Maybe they slowed Lachlan down," Frank said. "We've got to catch him!"

"We'd better do it fast," said Joe. "Check the fuel gauge." It was nearly on empty. "If we don't catch him in the next few minutes, it's all over."

Up ahead Frank spotted a silver gleam in the sky. On the amber windshield grid was a box labeled Image Enhancer. He moved this until it framed the silver dot, then hit the Enlarge Image command that appeared under the box. The box was suddenly filled by the piggyback 747–space shuttle combo. They were almost at the deadly rendezvous.

"Come on, Lachlan, where are you?" Frank demanded.

"Use this," Joe said, pointing to the image enhancer.

"Good idea." With the Enlarge command still in place, Frank moved the box all over the windshield, bringing every quadrant of the sky into close focus.

"There!" Joe shouted.

Max Lachlan had stuck to his ground-skimming tactic. The MAX-1 was racing along at nearly eight hundred miles per hour at an altitude of about fifty feet. He was just under ten miles away, according to the range finder.

"What's the range on the laser?" Joe asked.

"The light beam loses intensity in the air," Frank answered. "From this distance it'd be like hitting him with a flashlight beam."

He tracked the MAX-1 with his sights. For a split second it lined up in his crosshairs. He fired.

The beam of deadly light flashed out from the ship. It was right on target, but when it struck the MAX-1, it caused no damage.

"Well, at least it got his attention," said Joe. "Here he comes!"

The MAX-1 wheeled around and climbed toward them. Their radio crackled. Then Lachlan's voice snarled at them. "Is that you, Hardy? I'm going to get rid of you once and for all. Then I'll take out the president!"

"There's still time to give yourself up, Max. If you won't do it for yourself, do it for Moira's sake!"

Lachlan's response was a beam of light that streaked from the nose of his plane. But he wasn't yet in range. There was a thud, and the MAX-2 rocked, but it was undamaged.

Frank swerved the MAX-2 to the right, and the two craft began fighting like dragonflies, dipping and darting and hovering and whirling, each trying to gain the advantage. Beams of laser energy danced across the sky.

"Look! The president's plane!" Joe shouted.

He needed no magnifier to make out the details of the shuttle on top of the 747. They must know Max was out here, Joe thought. Why didn't they turn back to Edwards Air Force Base? The slow jumbo jet continued to draw closer.

Frank saw it, too, and knew that Lachlan must be calculating his chances of getting a shot at it. Frank knew he would have to finish this now, one way or another.

"Fuel's real low," said Joe. "We've only got minutes. Maybe not even that."

"Get out the jetpack," said Frank. "Put it on and get ready to bail out when I tell you."

"What about you?"

Frank gave him a fierce grin. "I'm going to be hanging on to you like I really love my little brother. And you'd better not lose your grip on me!"

As Joe struggled to get the jetpack on, Frank banked the MAX-2 around, then streaked straight for the MAX-1, firing. Lachlan fought back again, and the two planes wove an intricate, looping pattern.

Then one of the MAX-2's tail engines coughed and died. "That's it," said Frank. "Fuel's almost gone. Get ready to go."

The MAX-1 was on their tail, closing the distance. Lachlan wasn't firing. Frank knew he wanted point-blank range, to be sure of the kill.

When the MAX-1 was almost on top of them, Frank grabbed his brother and shouted, *"Now!"* He hit the canopy release, slamming back on the controls, and the MAX-2 stopped dead in midair. Then Joe fired up the jetpack, and they blasted up out of the MAX-2, hugging each other as they were carried away from the aircraft.

It took Max Lachlan a split second to realize what had happened. As he fired his laser, he saw that the MAX-2 was stalled, right in front of him. He tried to veer off, but it was too late. The instant after the beam touched the MAX-2, the MAX-1 plowed into it. The two exploded in a tremendous burst of flames, taking their maker with them.

"Hey, wake up, pal!" Frank Hardy shouted, bounding up the stairs to his brother's bedroom. "We've got mail—a letter from Moira."

Joe groaned and rolled over. He stared out the window. It was snowing again. Last time he'd seen Ray and Moira was in California.

Joe remembered that soon after he and Frank had landed after their battle with Max Lachlan, with just a few bruises and scrapes, the Network's Chinook helicopter had picked them up and taken them to Edwards Air Force Base. They spent a day there debriefing, along with Moira and her fiancé. Ray was okay, and Moira was holding up better than they'd expected, considering her father's death.

The next morning the Hardys were winging back home in a C-130 transport, courtesy of the United States Air Force. Ray and Moira saw them off. "We decided to stay here awhile," Ray had explained with a grin. "We could use a little sun and fresh air while we recuperate."

"I'll be back in Bayport eventually," Moira had assured them. "Dad may be gone, but Lachlan Air Design still has work to do." She looked determined, but her voice wavered. "I just can't do it now," she added. "Give Jill my love when you see her, and tell her I'm sorry she lost her story."

"*You're* sorry!" Joe winced. "Have you ever had to tell Jill Stern that the biggest scoop of her life is top secret?"

Lying in bed now, Joe grinned. Moira and Ray had looked happy together. In fact, they'd told the Hardys that they planned to be married before summer. "And you're going to be my best man," Ray had said, clapping a hand on Frank's shoulder. Then he'd looked at Joe. "Can a guy have *two* best men?"

Moira had managed a smile. "You can't have Joe Hardy," she'd teased her fiancé. "He's going to give away the bride."

Frank Hardy stood over his groggy brother, dangling the letter from their friend.

"Well?" Joe demanded. "What does she say? Are they happy, healthy, and tan? How's the surf?"

"Actually," said Frank, "she doesn't say anything, but she did send us something. This."

He handed a folded sheet of paper to his brother. Joe took one look and began to hoot with laughter.

Moira had photocopied an article from a Nebraska newspaper. Joe read the headline once more and fell back against his pillow, laughing uncontrollably. "Not the kid at the gas station!" he hooted.

His brother joined in, and the two of them roared with mirth.

The headline read, "Local Teen in Death Race with UFO—Lives to Tell the Tale!"

Frank and Joe's next case:

When Buddy Death brings his heavy metal band to Bayport, danger takes center stage. For while hard rock fans would kill for a ticket, someone's out to kill the star of the show! The Hardys, who've been hired to help set up the concert, soon find themselves working overtime as Buddy Death bodyguards.

But saving Buddy's skin is not an easy job, and Frank and Joe can't afford to miss a single beat. The hot-shot rock star has more enemies than he does amplifiers—and every piece of high-tech equipment onstage is a potential Buddy Death trap . . . in *Rock 'n' Revenge*, Case #48 in The Hardy Boys Casefiles™.